Praise for *A Woman's Persuasion*

"It is a tribute to Watts' sensitivity and skill that the narrative, while following the original story closely, holds plenty of tension and some cleverly engineered surprises... the whole thing is great fun as Watts brings Jane Austen's tale of yearning and missed opportunity bang up to date."
-Jocelyn Bury, *Jane Austen's Regency World*

"All the heart and humor of your favorite Regency romance but with a modern sensibility that truly allows love to triumph over every obstacle."
Miranda MacLeod, Author of the *Love's Encore* series

"An interesting, thought-provoking and sweet novel."
Maria Biajoli, Professor of English Literature, UNIFAL

A Woman's Persuasion

A Woman's Persuasion

Jeanette Watts

Copyright © 2019 Jeanette Watts

All rights reserved.

ISBN:9781691055548

To Charlie, my Air Force Expert:
Thanks to your patience, I'm not going to lose
all the officers in the audience.

To Nicole, for all the good advice and hand-holding.

And to Shirley
I will never, ever write another novel
without missing your guidance.
Wherever you are now,
caring soul that you are,
I know you're still looking out for me.

To James with love from one Janette to another! Jeanette

Special thanks also to H and S Antiques for allowing us to shoot the back cover in their beautiful store!

CHAPTER 1

Walter Elliot's favorite book was *Who's Who in America*. While most financiers might have preferred *The Wall Street Journal*, that was merely reading in order to get the day's news. That was work, not pleasure. Seeing his entry always gave him a boost on a bad day. On the other hand, it still gave him a boost of satisfaction and pleasure when he was having a good day.

ELLIOT, WALTER J.

Banker. **Personal:** Born Sept 28, 1954, New York, NY; son of James and Mary Elliot; married Elizabeth Steventon (deceased), January 5, 1979; children: Elizabeth, Anne, Mary. **Educ:** Cornell University, BA, 1976; Columbia Business School, MBA, 1978. **Career:** Union Savings and Loan, various positions, 1978-1993, Security Savings Bank, corp lending officer, 1993-1997, Washington Mutual Bank, loan analyst, 1997-1998, Prosperity Bank, assistant vice pres & mgr of credit admin, 1998-2001, Metro Bank, vice pres 2002-. **Orgs:** Columbia Univ Alumni 1979 -; mem Metropolitan Club, 1979; mem The Core Club, 2003 -. **Honors/Awds:** Cornell Univ Distinguished Alumni Award. **Business Addr:** Metro Bank, 29 Wall Street, New York, NY 10005.

A Woman's Persuasion

For a man of 54, he spent a lot of time looking in mirrors. He prided himself on being follicly gifted; he still sported a full, thick head of hair, and a judicious application of Just for Men meant that no one needed to know that there was a little bit of gray coming in at his temples. For all he knew there was a lot of gray, but since he kept the silver traitors carefully managed, he had no way of knowing how much was actually there.

He took as much trouble with his figure as he did with his hair, and maintained a membership at the most exclusive gym in Manhattan. He kept a membership for the entire family, so that his daughters could also maintain their figures and be a credit to him. His eldest, Elizabeth, was his favorite workout companion, and managed to keep herself to a size 6. His youngest, Mary, was married with children, and couldn't be expected to maintain her pre-baby size. But at least she managed to keep herself down to a size 10.

His middle daughter, Anne, drove Walter to the depths of despair. She would rather lay around with a book reading instead of coming to the gym with him and Elizabeth. She used to be just as slim as her sisters, but over the years, she just seemed to grow wider, and wider, and wider. She was something like a size 22 now. She was barely fit to be seen in public these days. She cared nothing about her appearance and refused to put on makeup when they were going out. When she did dress up, she looked like she was wearing a circus tent! He had offered her sessions with his personal trainer, but she refused until he stopped offering.

Walter had no idea where Anne got her fat from. The girls' mother Elizabeth (who always went by Liz) had been a size 2 when they met, and was never larger than a size 4. People had suggested to him that Anne was "stress eating." That was ridiculous. When his wife died, Anne hadn't swelled up like a pregnant woman in her 11th month. But at some mysterious time after that, she had stopped caring about her appearance, spent more time reading and eating and stopped doing anything that looked like exercise. It was disgraceful, how lazy she'd gotten. No matter what he might say or do to try to get her to have a care about what an embarrassment she was to him, she just insisted on shuffling around in her slovenly way.

Lanie Russell, Liz's best friend, also worried about Anne's weight. Anne was her favorite of Liz's children, being the only one of the girls who took after their mother in both looks and disposition. She had her suspicions as to when and why Anne had grown more than 10 sizes over the last 8 years, but she was unwilling to broach the subject with her goddaughter. Some things were best left in the past, and the less said, the better.

Elizabeth had too many interesting things to think about to waste any time worrying about her sister's dress size. So, Anne got fat. Lots of people got fat. Anne always preferred reading to exercise; of course if you sat around doing nothing you weren't going to stay the same size that you were in high school. Elizabeth worked at the same bank as her father, in the legal department, putting her law degree to good use. Working at the bank lost its luster for a painful period of time: she had dated her father's protégé, a promising young man who happened to share the same last name. But William Elliot seemed to be more interested in kissing up to her because she was the boss's daughter than he was interested in actually kissing her. When he left the bank for a better offer, she was less hurt than her father was angry. Which is not to say she wasn't very hurt. It's just that her father was that much more angry.

Fueling Walter's anger was the fact that when William left the bank, he was criticizing some very lucrative practices. Who didn't dabble in a few subprime mortgages, these days? Everyone on Wall Street did it. Sure, it was a higher-risk practice. If you couldn't stomach risk, you didn't belong in the financial industry.

But, of late, there was some movement in the market that would suggest that maybe William was a little bit right. More and more people seemed to be defaulting on their loans. And even though the bank had been processing more and more foreclosures, they couldn't seem to keep ahead of the falling profits. Shareholders in the bank were beginning to get restive, and Walter was starting to worry.

He had suggested to Elizabeth that, just in case, perhaps they ought to consider making a few changes to their plans, and keeping a bit more of their money set aside in case of something unthinkable happening. A few top people were being let go at firms up and down Wall Street. Mortgage-backed securities started an alarming plunge in value. The entire housing market continued to plummet. Elizabeth suggested they scale down the decorations at their annual Halloween party, and maybe hire a DJ instead of a band for the Christmas party.

Then the unthinkable happened: Lehman Brothers filed for bankruptcy. Eight more banks, including Walter and Elizabeth's, were expected to follow suit. Both Elliots had invested major portions of their savings in their own bank, and when the next quarter's statements came out, they had suffered massive financial losses.

"The Feds offered to step in and bail out AIG, surely they will bail us out as well," Elizabeth offered hopefully.

"As well they should!" Walter declared. "I'd like to see the country try to live without banks."

"If only stupid people would pay their mortgages, none of this would have happened," Elizabeth punched the arm of their leather sofa repeatedly, with increasing force, until her father stopped her.

"If the government doesn't bail us out, and our bank forecloses, we won't be able to afford to replace that couch," he cautioned her.

Elizabeth folded her arms and slouched down into the couch. "I don't see why people don't just pay their bills," she frowned.

"Well, now you can't pay yours, and you are going to need to drastically change your lifestyle," said Lanie Russell as she walked into the room, Anne Elliot behind her.

"Hello, Lanie, when did you get here?" Walter greeted her from where he was draped across his favorite leather recliner. "I didn't hear the bell."

"That's okay, Anne did." Lanie took the seat Walter indicated for her, next to Elizabeth on the sofa. Anne was disinclined to join the conversational group, and sat in the window seat and studied the trees across the street in Central Park.

CHAPTER 2

"Well, Walter," Lanie Russell was not the sort of woman who beat around the bush, "this is a pretty turn of events. Have people started jumping off buildings on Wall Street yet?"

Walter gave her a sour look. "Not yet."

"Not that I can blame people when they do start jumping," Elizabeth interjected. "What is this world coming to, when a bank can't do business without everyone in the world blaming them for problems that aren't their fault?"

"The securities industry has been thriving since they stopped hamstringing us with so many dammed regulations," Walter waved his hands expressively, if helplessly. "Why should we be the ones to suffer when something goes wrong? We've been foreclosing on houses and businesses as fast as we can process them. It's not our fault the system for foreclosure takes too long for us to keep up."

A small noise came from the direction of the window seat. If Walter and Elizabeth heard it, they were ignoring it. Lanie imagined she knew that Anne disapproved of her parent's heartless tactics, but did not feel inclined to voice any objections. Or, any objections she had were already voiced, to no avail.

"Well, assigning blame does you no good right at this moment. A far more pertinent question is, what are you planning on doing right now? I'm asking you both as your wife's best friend and as your tax consultant; how much money have you lost?"

Walter and Elizabeth both sagged like wet paper towels. "Millions," Walter admitted.

"So before you end up with plenty of your own bills that you can't pay, you should get out of here before things get any worse," Lanie said shrewdly. She had to sternly refrain from letting her eyes drift in Anne's direction; this was Anne's idea. Anne had invited her to present the notion to Walter and Elizabeth, knowing that if Anne were to present the idea herself, it would be rejected out of hand. "Do either of you still have your jobs?"

Walter and Elizabeth looked at each other uncomfortably. "We don't know yet," Elizabeth answered. "The word is they are going to be eliminating entire departments, and something like a fourth to a third of the bank will be let go."

"Then we wait to see if the rest of the bank survives at all," Walter sighed glumly.

"So the shrewdest tactic right now is to retreat and regroup," Lanie observed.

Walter gave her a disgruntled look. "What is that supposed to mean?"

"It means, Walter, that instead of waiting for the axe to fall on your neck, you should be proactive, and remove yourself from the environment," Lanie explained. "Either find a new job, or go to your bosses, and offer to leave New York and go work on reorganizing the bank. You tell them you're willing to make the heavy sacrifice. You're willing to leave the city to do damage control wherever they need you. Go to Chicago. Go to California. Go to wherever they need help. Do some research, find out what state has the highest rate of foreclosures, and offer to go there. Instead of becoming a victim, you'll come out of this mess looking like a hero."

Both Elliots spoke up at once. "Leave the city?!" Elizabeth protested, while Walter was looking appalled. "The Midwest? I could wind up in the Midwest?"

"Would you rather wait until you're evicted from this lovely place of yours, and you are put out on the curb like the trash?" Lanie asked.

"We won't be able to get a decent price for selling it," Walter grumbled.

"Since you were able to assume the mortgage from Liz's parents, it's not like you have to worry about breaking even," Lanie pointed out. "They paid more than half of it before they passed away. I should think Manhattan real estate immediately across the street from Central Park is not likely to drop by more than fifty percent."

"You really have thought this through," Walter acknowledged resignedly. "Well, damn it, I can't say you're wrong."

"More than that, you know I'm right," Lanie answered. "The best way to succeed is to be the first person to get to a place. When the masses figure things out and follow, the competition will be much fiercer."

Walter shifted impatiently in his seat. "Okay, damn it, you want to hear me say it, I'll say it. You're right. I'll talk to the board of directors tomorrow. We have a board meeting in the morning, anyway."

"There now, that wasn't so bad, was it?" Lanie smiled. "Just think, now you get to have a new adventure." She rose casually from her seat and walked over to Anne. "It looks like such a lovely day out there, come take a walk with me, Anne. Central Park is much more fun to walk in than it is to look at." She looked back at Walter and Elizabeth. "Would either or both of you like to join us?"

"At the pace Anne walks? Absolutely not," Elizabeth sneered. "Penny Clay will be coming over later, so we can go for a run. You have fun waddling along."

Lanie's smile never wavered. "I enjoy a walk in the park. I get to see so much more when the world isn't whizzing by while I'm wheezing between gulps on my inhaler. Come along, Anne."

Wordlessly, Anne rose from her window seat, and the two women left the room. It wasn't until they were safely in the elevator that Anne ventured to ask, "Do you think they'll take the advice?"

"We'll know tomorrow," Lanie said with a reassuring smile.

CHAPTER 3

The conversation with the board of directors went well. As predicted, Walter was hailed as a hero and a genius. By the end of the meeting, Walter himself was firmly convinced that the idea of leaving the city had been his in the first place.

While there was a great deal of talk about sending Walter to Nevada, the bank managers decided to send him to Ohio, where he would oversee matters for the entire southwestern corner of the state.

"It is a great deal cheaper down there!" Lanie Russell enthused upon her return visit, bringing with her a realtor named John Shepherd who had been highly recommended by some of her clients.

"But aren't there Southerners there?" Walter protested with a shudder. "They'll say things like 'y'all.' And eat grits. I don't know what grits are, but they don't sound like food. Even worse, they have something called sausage gravy. They must all weigh two hundred pounds, eating sauces made out of fat."

Lanie avoided the temptation to point out to him that almost all gravies are made out of a fat of some sort, and returned to her introduction. "Mr. Shepherd, here, may already have a buyer for you."

"Really?" Walter actually looked surprised and pleased for a moment.

"Yes, sir," John Shepherd seized the moment of surprised silence as an opportunity. "Senator Croft is looking for a place in the city, and I thought your apartment would be perfect. And I thought you would be pleased to know that your glorious dining room and living room would be continuing to entertain important people."

"A senator? So he would be entertaining politicians?"

"Senator Croft is a woman, father," Anne interjected softly.

"Even worse." Walter did not elaborate on why the gender of the senator made it worse. "These rooms, filled with politicians? Crooks and sleazeballs, the whole lot of them. Do I really have to sell my home to one of them? I suppose one of these days these rooms will end up on the news as part of some scandal."

"Well, it can't be much more scandal than you're facing right now," Lanie pointed out. The latest *Wall Street Journal* had listed several prominent people who were being let go, and Elizabeth's name had been among them. She had learned from the newspaper before the bank had told her she was being dismissed. There was a week of tears and threats and any other number of loud noises in the Elliot household, before Elizabeth calmed down over an admittedly generous severance package.

"Now I have TWO daughters out of work," Walter sighed. "It's a good thing I've decided to make this rather drastic move, or the entire family might be collecting unemployment."

"You will make a handsome profit from the sale, and of course the cost of living and the cost per square foot is SO much cheaper in Ohio," Lanie tried to redirect the conversation into more positive channels. "It might be one of the cheapest real estate markets in the country. Just think of it, you'll be able to buy a mansion down there. You can have four times as much square footage. Six times. Imagine, a castle for less than the cost of a penthouse suite here. You can buy a sprawling estate, and have everyone at your new place falling over themselves to get invitations to your parties."

Walter frowned a moment, but he was cheered at the prospect of being able to continue as an important personage, and for a lot less cost. "I hadn't thought about owning a country estate. I suppose I should be able to buy a plantation. That would be kind of amusing. But then it would probably be some musty old building, and I couldn't abide living in some old thing with a leaky roof."

"There is plenty of new construction in all the cities in Ohio," Mr. Shepherd reassured him. "Columbus, Cincinnati and Dayton are all thriving, despite the state of the financial industry."

"I hope so," Walter answered. "And I hope the cost of living is as cheap as you're telling me. You think this senator is going to be able to offer me a decent price? I am going to need every penny I can get from this place. I don't care if housing prices are dropping everywhere, and houses aren't worth as much as the mortgages. This is New York, not California."

"Leave that to me," Mr. Shepherd said firmly. "I promise I will get you the best price per square foot that can possibly be had. After all, anyone would consider themselves lucky to find real estate along Central Park!"

Walter stood up. "Well, then, let's get on with it. I assume you need photographs of all the rooms to show this senator?"

"That would be helpful, yes," Mr. Shepherd smiled. "Lanie, could I get you to hold onto my camera bag while I take photos? I'll probably need more than one lens to do justice to this place."

"You should start with the dining room, the light right now is quite perfect," Walter insisted.

Anne was glad when everyone had quit the room. She was also glad her father had such a poor memory for anything that had to do with her life. Of course he didn't know that Senator Croft was a woman, and a woman who had half-siblings who were much younger than her due to her father's second marriage, and one of those siblings had been in the same college as Anne.

A sigh escaped her, and she spoke to the empty room. "A few months from now, and she could be sitting in this window, looking at this same view."

CHAPTER 4

Cornell University was known for its business school, but halfway through her college career Anne changed her major to study English. And that was when she met Freddie.

Frieda Matilda Wentworth was tall and buff; the perfect blonde-haired, blue-eyed German valkyrie from mythology. Her parents had met and married in Germany while her father had been serving in Stuttgart. She spoke both English and German like a native, which was fitting for someone with dual citizenship. (Anne always teased her that she could hear a touch of German accent when she spoke English. It wasn't true, but it was fun to say it, anyway.)

Freddie and Anne had worked on a group project together for a writing assignment. Then Freddie, who was actually an engineering major in the ROTC program taking the class as a Gen Ed requirement, asked Anne to proofread her papers because Anne was a much better writer. Then they took a cinema studies class together, and started holding hands while they sat in the dark watching movies. And the relationship progressed from there. Freddie told her that she was bisexual, and had dated men as well as women, and explained that she loved people, not genitalia.

Freddie's parents had met and accepted her past girlfriends as well as boyfriends. After Anne received a warm and enthusiastic welcome from them, she was emboldened to introduce Freddie to her father and her sister Elizabeth.

Things did not go so well in the Elliot household.

At first, Walter did not understand Anne's meaning. Anne's sister Elizabeth did, and when she explained it to their father, there was a great deal of yelling. Anne was mortified. She apologized to Freddie for being forced to witness such scenes. Freddie just hugged her and said she was glad she had come along for the moral support.

A Woman's Persuasion

After Freddie had left, the yelling continued. It continued for the rest of spring break. In the end, Walter gave Anne an uncomfortable ultimatum. Either she break it off with Freddie, or Walter would cut off Anne's tuition for college, call the college to get her thrown out of school, and then throw her out of the house and cut her off from all financial support.

Anne thought briefly of accepting these terms and going to live with Freddie; but Freddie was a senior, in ROTC, and as soon as she graduated was going to be sent to Germany. The military liked people who spoke German like a native. They were useful.

When Lanie found out about the hullaballoo, she gently but firmly lectured Anne on the error of her ways, of the sins she and Freddie were committing, eternal damnation. By the end of the lecture Anne realized she was not only a lesbian, she was also an Atheist. But telling that to Lanie Russell would only alienate her. While Anne could not afford to alienate her father for financial reasons, she did not want to alienate a woman who had been a surrogate mother for emotional ones.

A nineteen-year old sophomore in English with asthma was not going to be able to get into any branch of the military, so Anne's ability to follow Freddie was zero. Someone who was more clever, or more headstrong, or less able to see the disastrous consequences that would come of striking out alone, might have taken the risk. But Anne had to admit she was none of the above. A lifetime of wealth and privilege had poorly prepared her for life as a homeless person.

Even worse, she realized that if she tried to follow Freddie into the military, or even just lived with her off base somehow, it would damage Freddie's military career if anyone found out. She knew Freddie was fearless, and would be willing to take the risk. But that left it up to Anne to be the cautious, prudent one.

So, despising herself the whole time, she broke up with Freddie.

At least, unlike her family, there was no yelling, no name calling, no insults, no Bible quotes, no threats. Freddie looked hurt, got up from her seat, and left.

Anne's heart and soul departed with Freddie's retreating back.

The grades on her final exams were dismal. Her job performance working at the library was so poor, she was dismissed before the end of the school year. She ignored invitations from friends to go to movies, or to meals, or to study together, until the invitations stopped coming.

Anne retreated into solitude, and larger and larger helpings of chocolate and potato chips. Not together, of course. But the satisfaction of grease and salt, or the special kind of high that comes from two scoops of double dark chocolate ice cream with chocolate chunks in it, would temporarily quiet the ever-present pain inside her head and heart.

It was an awful summer. Walter and Elizabeth dragged her off for a vacation in Mexico, which was when Anne discovered she was not the sort of person who liked lying on the beach getting a tan, and she could only go swimming for so long, and she didn't want any tattoos. Lanie brought Anne with her to all sorts of social engagements, and threw men at her, one after the other. Then the men would get her phone number from Lanie, and Anne had to deal with endless phone calls from persistent admirers whom she had zero interest in talking to. Eventually she stopped answering phones, and spent her Friday nights deleting the messages on the answering machine.

She did get forced into going on a blind date with an easygoing fellow from Brooklyn. Charles Musgrove was on the short side, with curly brown hair and a passion for every kind of sport that could be televised on ESPN. He ran a successful string of dry cleaning businesses all over New York. Anne wasn't interested in him romantically, but she liked him well enough to introduce him to her younger sister Mary. They hit it off on their first date, and got married a few years later.

While Lanie was throwing men at her, Anne looked at other women, and wondered about starting over with someone else. If she could find someone rich and powerful, a protector would make it irrelevant if her family cut her off financially and emotionally. But such a woman didn't seem to exist. And, Anne knew, she didn't want someone else. She wanted Freddie.

She mentally calculated how many people knew about her relationship with Freddie. Freddie's parents knew. Freddie's siblings must have known by that time that Freddie was bisexual, but Anne didn't know that for a fact. For all she knew, only the parents knew the truth about Freddie's preferences. Did Freddie tell her brother and sister about Anne? That depended upon whether they knew the truth about Freddie. If they did know, they probably knew everything. If they didn't know, they probably knew nothing.

In her own family, her father and Elizabeth knew about Freddie, but her sister Mary, who had gone on a spring break trip with her senior class instead of coming home, knew nothing.

It left Anne feeling particularly alone; she had no confidante with whom she could talk about Freddie without judgment. She wondered about confiding in Mary, but after all these years Mary would be hurt and angry that she hadn't been told eight years ago when everything was happening.

Perhaps it was just as well.

CHAPTER 5

Senator Croft loved the apartment at first sight, and immediately made an offer. Since the Elliot family had made no preparations for the move, closing was established for two months hence. Walter needed to depart immediately for Ohio, since the bank wanted him to get started right away. It was decided that Walter and Elizabeth would find an apartment immediately, and Anne would oversee the move out of Manhattan; after which, Mary insisted that Anne stay with them in Brooklyn for a few months.

"One of our managers is taking maternity leave. It would be perfect if Anne could come help us out until she gets back," Mary emailed everyone in the family. "She simply must help. Last time we needed someone temporarily, the person we promoted to manager was not only stealing from us, he was letting the other employees steal from us, too. We had to fire almost everyone at that location and start over. It was a nightmare!"

Elizabeth emailed back, rather than letting Anne speak for herself. "Of course Anne might as well stay here to help you. It's not like she has a job or anything, and we won't need her in Ohio."

Lanie had been included in the group email, and rejoiced at Anne's being able to stay in the city a little bit longer. She was not quite ready to part with her yet.

"Oh, she can stay as long as you want her," Walter answered. "I invited Penny Clay to come with me and Elizabeth to help us move in."

This started a long string of back-and-forth emails. "I thought you just said you didn't need Anne, but you need Penny?" Lanie asked with pointed frankness.

"Penny works out at the gym with us, and she can lift her own body weight. She will certainly be useful in helping us unpack," Elizabeth explained.

"The idea of Anne lifting her own body weight is ludicrous. She will be far more useful here with you, and with Mary. Of course she can run a dry cleaning shop," Walter had added.

Fortunately Anne had been grocery shopping that day, and there was a fresh carton of chocolate chip cookie dough ice cream in the freezer. She left the spoon inside the carton when she put it back in the freezer. She had a feeling she would be needing it again, soon.

When Elizabeth joined her in the living room, Anne debated with herself for a while, then decided to speak. "Are you sure you really want Penny coming along for this move?"

Elizabeth did not even look up from her BlackBerry. "Of course I do. She'll be a great deal of help. Father agrees, we can't do without her. Just like Lanie isn't ready to part with you yet."

Anne tried again. "Things are different outside the city. People are far more interested in other people's business than here in New York. They will make assumptions, and it might be uncomfortable when their assumptions are correct."

Now Elizabeth looked up from her device to frown at Anne. "What the hell are you talking about?"

Anne gave up and went for the direct approach. "So how do you feel about having Penny Clay as our stepmother?"

Elizabeth's stare turned incredulous. "You're imagining things."

Anne did not let her gaze fall away from her sister's eyes. "What do you suppose they are doing when you're not here with them?"

"The same things we do when I am here!" Elizabeth threw her BlackBerry down on the coffee table, and paced among the suitcases packed and ready to leave with her and Walter in the morning.

Anne thought about continuing the argument, but as she opened up her mouth to point out the obvious, she remembered one of her favorite professors telling her about the times she had been a counter protester at an anti-abortion rally in front of a women's health clinic. They had been told not to engage with the people shouting slogans in their face. "Never try to teach a pig to sing," they had been instructed. "It wastes your time, and annoys the pig." She lifted her eyebrow, and closed her mouth.

"What?" Elizabeth asked.

Anne tried not to smile at the comparison between Elizabeth and a pig. "Nothing. If you're right, nothing will come of it. If I'm right, maybe you'll get to be a bridesmaid. Time will prove one way or the other."

"You're out of your mind," Elizabeth chose to pursue the subject. "Father has stayed single all these years on our account."

"We're grown up now," Anne pointed out. "Maybe he's thinking he's done his duty, and now he wants to have some fun."

"Penny is my friend, that's all!" Elizabeth snapped. "Our father is always teasing her about her bad teeth, and you know he could never abide tattoos. Penny has four of them. And Penny isn't pretty enough for Father's taste."

"A pleasing personality goes a lot farther than what's on the surface," Anne disagreed. "And if Penny doesn't have an attractive enough face, she also spends so much time jogging with you and father, surely he's noticed she's got muscular arms and legs. That might be more important to him than a pretty face."

"You don't know what you're talking about, Father would never be with a woman with so many tattoos." Elizabeth sat back down and picked up her BlackBerry, ending the conversation.

Lanie agreed with Anne. "Good Lord, what are you going to do when that sycophantic little snake succeeds in marrying your father?" she asked the next time they were alone. "She'll spend everything in your father's checkbook in a year, then divorce him like she did her first husband and move on to greener pastures."

"Me? I will have a very good laugh at Elizabeth's expense," Anne answered.

"This isn't a laughing matter," Lanie scolded.

"Well, if you think you can influence my father out of his having an affair with his daughter's best friend, have at it," Anne offered. "I certainly have no influence with him. But Elizabeth will have something to say about it if and when this were to come out. I'd back Elizabeth over Penny, any day."

"Penny Clay is a very clever manipulator," Lanie cautioned.

"And Elizabeth would run her over in a dark alley in the middle of the night before she'd let Penny take her place as Father's favorite companion," Anne answered. "But this is all speculation. No use looking for troubles we can't fix. Trouble has an easy enough time finding us, anyway."

Lanie came over in the morning to say good-bye as Walter, Elizabeth and Penny loaded their suitcases into a newly-purchased car and started their drive to Ohio. When Walter insisted on lifting Penny's heavy suitcase for her, Anne and Lanie couldn't restrain themselves from sharing a significant glance.

"I will come pay you a visit as soon as you get settled," Lanie promised. "Manhattan isn't going to be the same without you!"

"Oh, come off it, there's one and a half million people on the island, someone out there will be willing to go to Broadway with you once in a while." Walter was not generally a demonstrative person, but he gave her a parting hug, nonetheless. It was a cold, fishy, half-hearted sort of hug, but it was due to Lanie as his deceased wife's best friend.

He nodded to Anne. "Elizabeth took care of all the paperwork so that you have power of attorney for closing and anything else you should need to sign on my behalf."

Anne smiled. "Goodbye, Father. Safe travels."
Walter got in the car with the girls, and they were gone.

CHAPTER 6

Anne was home to let in the housing inspectors, and the repairmen, then the painters, then the extra cleaning staff. She made trips to the consignment shops and Goodwill to dispose of her father's and sister's unwanted clothing. She donated a box of her mother's old costumes to one of the small off-Broadway theatre companies. She went through her books, finding an occasional duplicate, and a pile of titles that, if she was honest with herself, she was never going to read again.

She had everything well in hand when the movers came to empty the apartment. It was going to be easier to work on repairs to the ceiling in the dining room and kitchen after the furniture had been moved out. Walter and Elizabeth found a house in Ohio with surprising speed, and so there turned out to be no need to put their possessions in storage.

"Thank goodness for that," Lanie told her fervently. "There is nothing worse for one's things than to put them into storage."

Anne walked through the empty rooms after the movers had left, Lanie beside her, and the two shared a melancholy silence. Even after all these years, they could still feel the presence of Anne's mother. She used to love the window seat for reading. She would stand in front of the gas fireplace in the living room on cold days, and slowly rotate, so that she would warm up evenly. She baked so many Christmas cookies in that oven. She prided herself on their yearly Christmas party. She would try out new recipes every year, in case guests got bored eating the same goodies. Anne laid her face against the doorframe of the closet that had been her mother's. Her father had taken up the extra space after she'd died, but it was still her mother's closet. If she closed her eyes and breathed, she could imagine she could still smell her mother's scent.

They walked along wordlessly, taking turns wiping away tears. After seeing all the rooms one last heartbreaking time, there was nothing to do but close the door behind them. Anne's suitcases were loaded into Lanie's car, so that Lanie could drop her at Mary's house in Brooklyn.

While most people from Manhattan turned up their noses at Brooklyn, Anne liked it. There was more space, more breathing room, more children playing catch in the park or riding skateboards down the sidewalk. There was a wide variety of restaurants that were all open until at least 2:00 am: Chinese, Thai, Vietnamese, pizza, Greek, Mexican.

The Musgroves shared a four-story brownstone that was only a block from the subway station and two blocks from Prospect Park. It was situated in the middle of the block on a tree-lined street, snuggled between all the other pretty four-story buildings, all with a short set of steps up to the second-story entrance. The two-family home was split between Charles, Mary and their two children in the lower floors, and the rest of Charles' family in the upper floors.

It was a pretty old place, full of mahogany woodwork, hardwood floors, and fireplaces. Anne always enjoyed a visit to the place, which Mr. Musgrove had named Uppercross in honor of family he had found on his family tree back in England.

Unlike the ironic solitude of living in their apartment in Manhattan, Uppercross was always filled with people. Charles' younger brothers, Henry and Louis, could be popping downstairs after school. Mary's sons might end up sleeping upstairs with their uncles or grandparents. Meals might be eaten among the individual families, or everyone might congregate upstairs or downstairs or outside in the garden. It depended upon who felt like starting the grill on the patio, or who had made a fresh batch of pasta sauce that afternoon.

Knowing the communal nature of Uppercross, Anne was surprised to find Mary alone when Lanie dropped her off. She was in the kitchen, stirring a pot full of something with her left hand, while texting on her phone with her right hand. She was so startled by Anne's arrival, she nearly dropped the phone into the pot.

"It's about time you got here!" She handed Anne the large wooden spoon. "Here, keep stirring this. I nearly burnt it. I should get rid of Mother's Hungarian goulash recipe. It burns much too easily." She handed Anne the spoon, and began using both hands to continue texting.

Anne turned down the heat on the stove, and continued stirring Mary's large pot full of beef and tomatoes and potatoes and peppers and paprika. She sniffed the contents and smiled. It smelled like their childhood.

"I didn't think you were ever going to get here. Why couldn't you be here a week ago? I've been having to cover the shop in Midwood by myself, and I'm going to tear my hair out."

Anne could feel the burned goulash on the bottom of the pot, and stirred more gently to not introduce the burned parts into the rest of their dinner. "Last week you texted that you were fine, and I didn't need to hurry on your account."

"I was lying, you idiot!" Mary was talking and texting at the same time. "I was trying to be nice. I didn't think you had that much left to do, so I didn't tell you to hurry. But I've been left to run three shops on my own, and I desperately need you. Especially now, during football season. You know how Charles is when the Giants are winning. So, Lanie couldn't even bother to get out of the car long enough to say hello when she dropped you off?"

"You know Lanie," Anne excused her, "she's always got eight hours of commitments and six hours with which to fulfill them. Of course she sent love and hugs when she dumped me at your doorstep."

"I've hardly seen her all summer," Mary grumbled. "But then I don't suppose she would have much use for me. I don't have time to play, I'm a working woman with a string of dry cleaners to keep running."

Anne ignored the complaints about her friend, who was also a working woman, and redirected her sister. "Well, I do hope Charles runs the dry cleaning business, and you help him out."

"Oh, Charles is no help. I swear, I have no idea how he managed to own so many branches without me. He's never around to talk to me about whether he wants to continue putting coupons in direct mail, or if he wants to try advertising online somehow. He's opening another location in Bay Ridge. I asked him to make time to talk to me before he left this morning, but he ran out to go over the site with the real estate agent. But I don't know how he expects to run another branch when he doesn't manage the ones he already has. He spends all his time at football games."

"Well, you know we always manage to keep everything running. I took over for you when you had Charlie, and again when you had Walter. Just think what we can do together." She changed the topic. "How is everyone upstairs? I'm amazed we haven't seen anyone yet."

"My father-in-law stopped down this morning to collect a charging cord he left here last night, otherwise everyone went off to work and school first thing this morning." She put down her phone to check the video camera showing Walter awake from his nap and starting to cry. "Oh, Anne, why couldn't you have been here earlier? You would have kept me from tearing my hair out if you could have been here last Thursday."

"Last Thursday you said I needn't hurry on your account," Anne reminded her. "And I had so much to do getting ready for the movers, I am not sure how I could possibly have come any earlier."

"Oh! Moving isn't nearly as difficult as people make it out to be." Mary handed her a stack of bowls to set next to the pot.

"I assure you, I've had plenty I needed to take care of," Anne protested. "Besides the logistics of everything that needed to be repaired, packed, given away, or otherwise dealt with, I'm also leaving our home. Can you imagine not being able to walk in Central Park anymore?"

"Of course I can," Mary gave her a dirty look. "How often do you suppose I've walked in Central Park since I got married?"

"Every time you came up to see us," Anne said. "You could always have come more often than you did, you know. It's not that long of a subway ride."

Walter was serious about crying now, and Anne elected to retrieve her nephew while Mary sliced bread to serve with the stew. "I wish crock pots came in larger sizes!" she complained when Anne came back, bouncing Walter on her hip. "I don't mind taking my turn at feeding the whole clan, really I don't, but I do wish I could just throw everything into a crock pot and plug it in."

The sisters put the heat on low and covered the sliced bread with a napkin, pulled out the stroller, and were leaving the house for a quick walk in Prospect Park when the Musgroves arrived. Henry and Mrs. Musgrove were walking home together, having ridden the same subway. Henry was in school at Columbia; he took the number one red line to the Chambers Street stop, and always waited for his mother so that they could finish the journey together. Louis was in law school at NYU and tended to get home later than the rest of the family; so it was a pleasant surprise when he called a greeting from across the street not ten minutes later, while they were all still out front talking.

The Musgroves held a certain fascination for Anne. The entire family could argue, talk over each other instead of listening to each other, and the parents frequently protested they simply could not understand their children; but they really and truly liked each other. The love and respect they showed each other daily never failed to warm Anne's heart, chilled as it was by her own relationships with her sisters and father. She never quite envied them, but she very much enjoyed their banter, and the way they always welcomed and included her as a member of the family.

It was a full half hour before they had finished greeting Anne, talked to each other, and concluded it was time to go inside. Mary and Anne's walk in the park was postponed until after dinner, when several of the Musgroves elected to join them. After all, it looked like it was going to be a chilly but otherwise pleasant night.

CHAPTER 7

Dinner was a merry affair. The goulash was consumed with much appreciation, and most of the family lingered after dinner to tell stories about their days, tell Anne again how glad they were to see her, and to talk about the Giants.

Over the next few days, everyone seemed to find some time to talk to Anne alone. They confided to her their complaints about her sister, and her sister confided her complaints about them.

"Charlie is a menace! And now that Walter is walking, he's working on becoming just as bad," Mrs. Musgrove complained.

"I'm not much of one for kids, so I'm a fine one to talk, but I'm a pretty big guy. So when I say Charlie is a bit much to handle, I'm not just being a wuss," Henry confided. "I babysat the other day, and when he decided he didn't want to take a bath, well, I ended up completely drenched. I had to tell Mary I won't babysit for her anymore. It's not that I don't love my nephew, but I'm not doing that again."

"I do wish Mary would let us take the children to daycare," Charles senior muttered to her. "She's hopeless at running the dry cleaning business with the distraction of both the boys, and the boys aren't getting very good parenting because of the distraction of the dry cleaning business."

"I had no idea that being a parent was going to be so hard," Mary sighed to her when she stopped by the dry cleaners that was under Anne's care. Little Charlie was running around underfoot and Walter was crying because he couldn't keep up with his brother. Charles junior had just turned four, and required constant supervision. He had a talent for finding someplace he wasn't supposed to be, or something he wasn't supposed to be doing. Mary's exasperated scoldings merely made him laugh. After a fourth incident that found him climbing to the top of a garment rack, Anne kept him busy with her in the office, sorting pens, pencils, and paper clips. A quick walk down the street to the art supply shop, and she was able to keep him busy with crayons and coloring books.

"I see why he obeys you better than me," Mary observed resentfully as she closed the office door after she put Walter down for a nap. "You bribe him with things he likes to do. We've got an entire cabinet full of toys here for him, I don't see why he can't play with those."

Anne opened the cabinet doors and examined the contents. "When was the last time you brought the boys anything new for this cabinet?"

"New?" Mary frowned at her. "What's wrong with the toys they have in there?"

Anne pulled out the first few toys at the front of the cabinet. "I bought these for Charlie when he was younger than Walter. I think developmentally they've both outgrown them. They might like a bigger challenge than toys that tell them that ducks say 'quack' and cows say 'moo.'"

"I want a duck that says 'moo' and a cow that says 'quack,'" Charlie declared from where he was busily coloring on the floor.

Anne smoothed out the large sheets of packing paper from the box of supplies she was unpacking, and handed them to her nephew. "Why don't you draw them for me? There's enough paper here, you can draw an entire farm for me."

Charlie grinned up at her and took the offered canvas for his artwork, and managed to occupy himself with his farm artwork for most of the afternoon.

While the days were full of children and dry cleaning, nights at the Musgrove family brownstone were always full of people and laughter. The Musgroves had the biggest living room of all their friends, with furniture easily moved out of the way, and a fondness for teaching swing dancing whenever they were called upon. And they were called upon frequently. There were swing dances every Friday night down at Trinity Grace Church, and lessons on Mondays and Tuesdays elsewhere in Brooklyn, but there was always a frustrated student who wanted some extra help, or a collection of students who wanted more practice at something they had learned in class.

It was not unusual for a lesson to turn into an impromptu dance. The brothers would join in, and next door neighbors could be called up if there was a gender imbalance, and soon the room would be full of dancers.

Anne would dance a little to please the Musgroves, then declined as soon as she was able to extricate herself. While she didn't generally suffer too much from a lifetime of asthma, the rigors of swing dancing quickly left her gasping for air. In order to participate in the festivities, she would man the keyboard that normally lived in the closet, and played boogie woogie songs. Fortunately swing music did not require one have the voice of an opera singer, and most of the time the entire room sang along with her while she played "Boogie Woogie Bugle Boy," or anything by Jerry Lee Lewis.

The days and nights passed fairly pleasantly between the dry cleaners and the Musgrove house; until suddenly September 29th was upon them, and it was the day to close on the apartment in Manhattan.

Anne had been surprised when her father gave her power of attorney to handle the details of closing on the house. Then again, since he declared it was a terrible inconvenience for him, perhaps it wasn't such a surprise, after all. Mary insisted on accompanying her into Manhattan for the closing, saying it would be nice to take the boys on an outing. Anne suspected she was peeved for not also being given power of attorney, and came along just in case she was needed to sign something for some reason. She pointed out that a closing was a lot of time sitting in an office signing papers, but Mary would not be deterred and got out the double stroller.

When they showed up at Mr. Shepherd's real estate office to sign the papers, the Crofts were already there, telling the lawyers stories and making everyone in the room laugh. Senator Sophie Croft was even more charismatic in person than she seemed on television; she exuded warmth and confidence. She was a person who made things happen, and if events didn't go her way, she would roll up her sleeves and work to change things until they *did* go her way.

Her husband Adam, Anne gathered, had been a lawyer for the Air Force, and had recently retired from service to start a civilian career. He was the reason they were moving to New York City: he had just joined a large law firm in town.

He also, apparently, had a way with children. While Charlie was more likely to look at things in a room, Walter tended to check out the people. As soon as Mary had taken him out of the stroller in the waiting room of the real estate office, he looked around, and started walking straight for Adam Croft. "Well, hello, there, little fella," he said when Walter gripped onto his knees. "You coming to visit us? You're certainly not the shy sort, are you?" Walter grinned up at him, and reached out a hand.

"Watch out for your glasses," Anne warned him. "He loves glasses."

"Oh, is that it." Mr. Croft put out both his hands. "You want to come up and get a better look?"

As he was lifting Walter to sit on his knee, Charlie came over to investigate whom his brother had found that was so interesting. "Hello!" Adam greeted his new visitor. "Do you belong to him?"

"He's my brother," Charlie explained.

"Charlie, Walter, you shouldn't be bothering the nice man," Mary scolded them.

"Oh, we're fine," Adam assured her. "We might as well play while we are waiting for the conference room to be ready for us."

Naturally, it was at that exact moment that Mr. Shepherd came to announce that the conference room was ready, and invited them to get started. Anne ended up walking down the hall next to Senator Croft.

"You've lived in the city all your life?" the senator asked Anne.

"I was born right here in Manhattan," Anne confirmed.

"This must be very difficult for you," she paused to let Anne pass through the door first.

"It is," Anne answered simply.

"I hope you end up liking your new home," Senator Croft smiled at her encouragingly. "I have a sister in the Air Force who is stationed out at Scott Air Force Base in Illinois. That can't be too far away, can it? It's all in the Midwest. She says it's nice out there. She's at McGuire Air Force Base in New Jersey for some training classes right now, but she's been in Illinois for the past couple years, I think. She says she's going to come visit me, since I'm only a couple hours away, now."

Senator Croft might have asked why Anne was suddenly beet red, but at that precise moment, Mary's sons came wailing in, angry that they had been separated from their newfound friend. All attention was focused on the small boys, giving Anne time to compose herself before Mr. Shepherd came in. Mary ushered the boys out, and the signing of the paperwork commenced.

CHAPTER 8

It was inevitable that the process of moving out of any place lived in for so many years would be complicated. Anne spent the next week exchanging text messages with Adam and Sophie Wentworth. How to work the dishwasher and the dryer. The trick for opening the doors to the little balcony. Where the breaker box was hidden. She was appalled at the number of little things she had not thought to write down. And it was funny, the items that got left behind. A pair of pants found in the back of the built-in cabinet. An entire drawer full of gadgets left in the kitchen.

> I do feel like an idiot, I obviously didn't check the kitchen very well after the movers packed.

Anne replied to the text about the drawer's contents.

> It's well hidden, but it's not like I didn't know it was there. I am making one last visit to my dentist, so I will be in Manhattan tomorrow afternoon. I can stop by, if you want to throw everything into a bag and leave it at the front desk.

That would be fine.

Sophie Croft had written back. (She had insisted that Anne stop calling her "Senator" all the time.)

> I will be gone, but my sister is staying with us! Her training got postponed, and she's got nothing to do but cool her heels for a week or two. So she's taking leave and helping us move in. Apparently she has a ton of leave saved up! I will let her know you are coming by sometime in the afternoon. Here's her phone number. Just text when you are coming, and she will bring your stuff down to you.

Anne stared at the words on her phone. She was here. Freddie was now here, in New York. Of course the Senator wouldn't know that there was a reason that Anne couldn't go to collect their things from Freddie. But she had no idea how on earth she would ever manage to avoid the meeting.

The next day, little Charlie turned out to be her savior, in the most awful way possible. Mary had brought the children with her to the dry cleaners, as always, even though she and Charles senior had another argument about putting the children into daycare. (That was the problem with living in such close quarters in a house anywhere in the city of New York – there were no secrets among family members.) While Anne was in the back, and Mary was at the counter taking care of customers, Charlie climbed up the garment racks again, and in the process of trying to get onto an even higher perch, he had fallen.

The paramedics were called, and Charlie was carefully examined, then just as carefully transferred onto a stretcher. He had dislocated his collarbone.

Mary was a basket case. "I only looked away for a moment! If Mrs. Cohen would have spent a little less time telling me about her dog, I would have been there before he had climbed up quite so high."

Anne thought about pointing out that Mrs. Cohen had left the building several minutes before Charlie took his unfortunate tumble, but she didn't think it would do any good. "You ride with him to the hospital, I'll mind the shop until closing time. Do you want me to keep Walter with me and take him home, or do you want to keep him with you?"

Mary stared at her. "I don't want to go to the hospital. Can't you go, instead?"

"I don't have the insurance cards and so forth. It's better if you go with him, you're his mother," Anne pointed out.

"I can't handle this. Why didn't I have girls?" Mary wailed.

"Because the Universe is giving you a little more than you can handle, just to make you tougher," Anne answered.

A Woman's Persuasion

Charlie was placed in the ambulance, Mary was assisted inside, and the doors were closed after she gave Anne one last mournful look. Walter cried for his mother for a brief moment, then cheerfully forgot about her when another customer came into the store, with two Shiba Inus on leashes.

She had the presence of mind to call to postpone her dentist appointment, and then stared at her phone. Sophie Croft had sent her Freddie's phone number in a group text, introducing them. Her thumbs hovered above the keypad on her phone.

> Can't come collect my things today, my nephew is on his way to the emergency room right now. I have to stay to close down our shop and take care of my other nephew.

Sophie answered several minutes later.

> Sorry to hear about your nephew! We will keep the bag in the front closet until you are able to collect it. Just let us know.

There never was a text acknowledgement from Freddie.

The next day, however, another text from Sophie (only to Anne this time) arrived to retie the knots that were just starting to loosen in Anne's stomach.

> Hey, we're throwing a little house warming party. I don't suppose you and your sister would like to come? You can pick up your stuff, and while you're at it, you might like to meet some of the guests. Andrew Lloyd Webber is in town, and plans on coming. Carrie Underwood has also promised to stop by. I'd also love to introduce you to my sister Freddie!

Anne wandered around with her phone in her pocket for over an hour before she finally texted back.

> That sounds amazing! It's going to depend on how my nephew is doing. If he's all right I would love to come. And my sister will be over the moon. She loves country music. I can

> confidently RSVP for her, too. If it's not too much to ask, may I bring her husband, too? He is an even bigger fan of Miss Underwood than my sister.

> By all means, bring any family members you like. Especially if they're voters ;-p

There were so many distractions in the Musgrove house, with Charlie home from the hospital with his arm in a sling and strict instructions to keep him relatively inactive for a couple of weeks. As the sedation wore off, the little boy was more and more fussy, unhappy with his food, with the entertainment options, with his sling, with the world in general. It took Anne a couple of hours to tell Mary about the invitation. As she guessed, her sister was ecstatic.

"Carrie Underwood?! In our apartment? That's amazing!"

Anne was more intrigued by the notion of meeting Andrew Lloyd Webber, but she didn't say anything. She realized of course her sister had no idea who Andrew Lloyd Webber was. And she wasn't sure there was any enticement under the sun that could overpower her dread of seeing Freddie again.

Charles' excitement tipped the balance in favor of going. The moment he walked in the door, he shouted her name, and wrapped his arms around her in an ecstatic bear hug, and picked her up off the floor. "I can't believe you're going to get us to meet Carrie Underwood! I really can't believe this!"

He had barely let go of her when Henry and Louis came in. "Where is Anne?! Where is our new BFF?!" They crushed her between them in a double bear hug, and jumped up and down with her, whooping with excitement and singing "I ain't spending no more time Wasted!"

"You are amazing! Only you would manage to get us the chance to meet real live famous people," Louis kissed her on the side of her forehead.

"Hey! If you're doing that, I want the other side." Henry also planted a kiss on her head. Then they both squeezed as hard as they could.

"How long do we have to make ourselves pretty before we have to leave?"

"We should try to leave in about an hour," Anne answered.

As the time for departure approached, however, a snag developed in their plans. They had counted on Mr. and Mrs. Musgrove to babysit the boys for the night, but neither Charles nor Mary had thought to ask them. When they did not show up long after everyone expected them, Charles called his mother. He discovered his parents were both at a fundraiser in New Jersey, and wouldn't be home until very late. Even if they wanted to, they couldn't leave immediately: they had ridden with other friends and didn't have their own transportation.

The entire party, jubilantly buoyant moments ago, fell into shocked silence.

"Well, it's not like we all have to miss out," Louis pointed out. "Anne can take me and Henry, while you guys stay home with your sons."

"We both don't need to stay behind," Charles protested. "My son's doing all right. If Mary stays with him, I can still go."

"Why should it fall on me? You can stay here with your son," Mary protested indignantly.

"You're his mother," Charles pointed out.

"Well, you're his father," Mary snapped back. "You can take fifty percent of the responsibility for him."

"Why don't you both stay behind with him, he's your kid," Henry piped in.

Anne hesitated for a moment, then stated the obvious. "I'll stay with him."

All the Musgroves were so busy glaring at each other, at first none of them heard her. Then Mary looked at her. "What did you say?"

"The lot of you go, I'll stay here with him," Anne said, running a hand through Charlie's hair and smiling at him. He smiled back. She felt sorry for him. She knew something about what it was like to have parents that didn't seem to care much about you.

"You can't do that, you're the one with the invitation. You have to take us to the party," Henry said.

"Senator Croft met Mary, too. I'm sure she'll let you in if Mary goes," Anne answered.

"That doesn't seem right," Charles looked unsure.

"Why wouldn't that be okay?" Mary demanded. "I'm as much Father's daughter as Anne is, even if Anne was given power of attorney, not me. Senator Croft invited everyone in the family, didn't she, Anne?"

All Anne could think about was getting out of having to see Freddie. "Mary's right. She invited everyone. She did say everyone in the family was invited. That's why I could even bring you lot." She smiled at Henry and Louis.

Charles shook his head. "It's just not right. Mary, you stay home with Charlie, the rest of us will go. I'll come home early, and then you can go to the party."

Charlie settled the matter for everyone. Realizing what arrangements were being made, he threw his good arm around Anne and began screaming. "Auntie Anne! Wants Auntie Anne! You go way, I wants Auntie Anne!"

When his father tried to pull his son off of Anne, he clung to her and cried all the harder. When his face started turning from red to blue, both parents looked helplessly at Anne.

She looked calmly back at them. "It seems Charlie has made the choice for all of us. You go, I'll stay here and have a discussion with him about respecting his parents."

Charles frowned. "Are you sure? It really doesn't seem right."

"Well, either Mary or I have to go, we're the only ones the Senator will recognize. So Mary needs to go if I don't. And you're a bigger fan than Mary is, it seems a shame for you to miss the chance," Anne reasoned.

"That's a good point," Mary agreed. "Anne isn't a country fan, she doesn't need to go."

"You just need to remember to collect the bag of things we left behind," Anne reminded her. She made a mental sigh at the thought of missing the chance to meet Andrew Lloyd Weber, but the glee at dodging Freddie made it hard for her not to look eager to be rid of the lot of them.

Now that the decision was made, Henry and Louis were impatient to leave. "We'll remember," they promised, pushing Charles and Mary towards the door.

CHAPTER 9

Charlie, Walter and Anne spent a quiet night, watching Disney movies, reading books, eating pizza. After Walter fell asleep, and Charlie was still too uncomfortable to fall asleep, Anne taught him the 100 Bottles of Beer on the Wall song. She wondered vaguely how much her sister would hate her for that. But it seemed like her duty as a proper aunt.

After Charlie sang himself to sleep, Anne listlessly browsed the family movie collection. Besides the extensive Disney movies, there were hundreds of crime thrillers, chick flicks, horror films, courtroom dramas, anime, and comic book movies. Anne wasn't sure what she wanted, but nothing here seemed to suit her. She wanted an old Hollywood musical, or some classic like *Casablanca* or *Gone With the Wind*. Or maybe a Ken Burns documentary. Just the soundtrack to *The Civil War* would be soothing to her raw nerves.

She had to dig through piles of toys on the floor and all the cushions of the couch to find the cable TV remote. She finally found an old Cary Grant movie on Turner Classic Movies, made herself a cup of herbal tea with plenty of honey and found a fresh package of Oreos in the cabinet, then settled down on the couch to watch.

As soon as she figured out the movie she was watching was *Kiss and Make-Up*, there were loud, laughing voices at the front door, and the Musgroves came bursting into the living room.

"Anne! Are you still awake? We thought you'd have gone to bed," Charles surprised her by greeting her with a kiss. Well, maybe it wasn't much of a surprise. She could smell the alcohol on his breath. Looking around, she could see that they'd all been drinking quite a bit.

"Of course I stayed up to hear about the party," she lied. She had no idea what time it was. She snuck a glance at the bank of electronic equipment by the television. Nothing had the time clock set.

"It was fabulous! Carrie was only there for a little while, but we all got her autograph," Mary giggled. "She signed our coats, so we can wear her autograph next to our hearts!" She unbuttoned hers, and flipped one side so she could show Anne the signature scrawled in Sharpie on the lining.

Anne dutifully admired everyone's signatures on their coats. "Was Andrew Lloyd Webber there, as well?"

"Who? Oh, probably. There was some British guy there that people were making a fuss over," Henry shrugged. "But there was this girl there from the Air Force that we were busy talking to."

"Her name is Freddie," Louis jumped in eagerly. "She's a captain, and a pilot, and this tall, gorgeous kickass goddess!"

"She's more of a valkryie than a goddess," Henry was digging out his cell phone. He had one of the new fancy Apple phones that could take pictures and do all sorts of other things, and he poked at the screen a few times. "Look at her!"

Anne clenched her teeth together and dutifully looked at the screen. There was Henry, standing with his arm around Freddie. She looked buff, and blonde, and her cheekbones were sculpted and beautiful in the way they always were when she smiled.

Henry pulled up another picture, and she made a show of examining it, as well. Freddie was laughing in this one. Louis and Henry were enthusiastically chattering away, bragging about getting Freddie's phone number. She couldn't hear the words, she was merely glad she wasn't really required to contribute anything to the conversation. Her throat was so constricted, she wouldn't have been able to make any sounds.

It was a relief when Charles and Mary demanded her attention so they could tell her a word-by-word replay of meeting Carrie Underwood, of everything Carrie said and did from the moment she walked in the door until the moment she left. What she wore, how she looked. Then they told her what they ate, what they drank, how the apartment looked with someone else's possessions in there. It was hard to track any of it, since they were both talking at the same time. But it didn't matter. It gave Anne a chance to regain some of her composure.

"Did you thank Sophie Croft for bagging up our things? Where's the bag of our stuff?" she asked when they happened to both stop for a breath at the same time.

Everyone in the party looked surprised, and then sheepish. "I guess we forgot in all the excitement," Charles admitted. "Sorry."

"We have Freddie's phone number, we'll ask her tomorrow," Henry said.

"It gives us an excuse to text her!" Louis positively giggled like a schoolgirl, and then the two boys high-fived each other. Anne stared at them, stupidly. She wanted to tell them their crush was pointless, but at the same time, it was pointless to say anything. When nothing came of it, they would move on to other girls. Besides, her throat had closed up again, she couldn't have said anything if she wanted to.

CHAPTER 10

After a sleepless night, Anne got up early enough to run to the corner market for some Gatorade and bananas to combat the inevitable hangovers, and made breakfast for everyone. She texted the other half of the Musgrove family to invite them for brunch.

They all staggered into the dining room in pairs. Only she and little Walter did not look the worse for wear, since even Charlie was uncomfortable from his medical misadventure.

The voices in the room were a low murmur, punctuated by occasional gasps of pain when Walter would let loose with the sort of loud, happy squeal that only toddlers can make. Mary tried to get him to take a pacifier to keep him quiet, which only resulted in more loud noises, this time of protest. Anne had better success distracting him with goldfish crackers while everyone else set the table and helped themselves to the eggs and bacon and toast and butter and fruit Anne had set up buffet style on the sideboard.

A new loud noise contributed to the discomfort of the group when Louis' phone chirped, and Louis stood up with a triumphant shout upon reading the message. "It's from Freddie!" His hangover forgotten, he read the text out loud with a happy laugh. "You forgot your sister's bag of things last night. Do I remember that you live in Brooklyn? I'm going to the aquarium this morning, do you want me to bring it to you? Leaving soon, let me know, I'll need your address."

He did a happy dance around the dining room while his brother looked crestfallen, and the rest of the family moaned and covered their ears. Mrs. Musgrove finally protested. "Can you please keep it down to a dull roar? Your father and I can't recover from our party as quickly as you can recover from yours."

Louis was too busy texting his reply to do more than nod. While everyone else sat down to eat, he paced the room staring at his phone until the phone chirped again with an answering text. He made another noise to make most of the room wince. "She's on her way, she'll be here soon!" he crowed.

Anne had a plate full of eggs and bacon and toast, but suddenly found she couldn't swallow any of it. She tried some tea. That wasn't going down too well, either. She sat in her chair, watching her food getting cold, and continued handing goldfish crackers to Walter.

Even though the doorbell was expected, she still jumped when it rang. Henry beat Louis to the door to answer it, and in walked Freddie. "Wentworth Delivery Service!" Louis took the offered bag of lost kitchen paraphernalia, then Henry offered his arm to escort Freddie into the dining room.

"So, you know my brother and his wife Mary, this is my mom and dad. These are my nephews. Charlie is the one who managed to fall and dislocate his shoulder," Henry jumped in to make the introductions. "And this is Mary's sister Anne."

"So this is the brave little fella who took a tumble," Freddie's blue eyes smiled down at the little boy as she held out her left hand so he should shake with the one that wasn't in a sling. "Don't worry, lad, you will be back to climbing things you shouldn't in no time." She looked back up at the rest of the room, and her eyes met Anne's. It was probably no more than a second, but it felt like an hour. "I think we went to Cornell together."

It was Anne's turn to be casual. "I think you're right. English class, wasn't it?"

"That sounds right. Small world." At that point, Walter demanded Freddie's attention, pulling on her sleeve and offering goldfish crackers. The bright blue eyes stopped boring into Anne's soul and focused on the small boy. "Is that for me? Why, thank you."

Henry and Louis were getting impatient with not having Freddie's undivided attention. "So you're going to the aquarium by yourself? You want company?"

Freddie smiled, and Anne thought that everyone in the room stopped breathing. Freddie could have been a fashion model instead of a pilot if she had wanted. "I'd love the company. My sister and brother-in-law were busy today, and I didn't want them feeling guilty leaving me alone with their boxes of things to unpack. I told them I could certainly entertain myself, and figured they would stop fussing over me if I went and did something touristy. I've never been to the aquarium. It seemed like a good way to spend the day, and get out of the crowds. Manhattan can be an awful lot of people."

"Well, then, let's go!" There was a flurry of activity while first Henry, then Louis, ran upstairs to get coats, then the three of them were out the door.

After they left, the rest of the party finished their coffee and tea and the last of the Gatorade. Charles and Mary decided to put both boys in the double stroller and take a walk in Prospect Park, and Mr. and Mrs. Musgrove excused themselves with errands they needed to get done. So Anne faced the table full of dirty dishes and the sideboard full of brunch remnants alone.

Well, the moment she had dreaded had come and gone, and she didn't have to dread it anymore. They had made eye contact, words had been exchanged. And she wasn't dead. It hadn't killed her. She might have thought it would, but it didn't. She crunched on a leftover piece of cold bacon, calculating how many years it had been since they had stood together in the same room.

She had graduated in 2001, so it must have been 1999. Almost eight years. How can this possibly hurt so much, when there were almost eight years between their breakup and today? That was nearly a third of her life.

She tried to imagine what Freddie must be thinking. Eight years of military service; how many things had she done, how many adventures had she been on, how many other women had she met? How much had she changed from all the experiences she'd had?

She remembered the bright blue eyes boring into hers in those few awful and precious seconds. She was still the same beautiful, driven, brilliant woman she'd fallen in love with. Then she remembered the way she received Henry and Louis' attentions, and part of her had to wonder. Had the military changed her, forced her back into the closet? After all, the military liked to enforce a rather conservative view of the universe. She might be willing to pretend to be something she was not, for the sake of her career.

It was a relief when Charles and Mary and the boys got home from their walk. It was hard to hear herself think with their four voices filling the air.

It was less of a relief late that afternoon, when Henry and Louis got home from the aquarium, full of news of everything they did, and everything Freddie said. "We tried to get her to come back here with us. We promised her dinner, but she already had plans. She did agree to take a rain check, so we'll get to see her again sometime soon. She was thinking maybe we can meet her in Manhattan."

Anne understood the conversation completely: Freddie was trying to avoid her. "Maybe it's just as well, you don't want to monopolize TOO much of her time."

"Oh, yeah, we asked her what you were like in college," Henry amended the earlier narrative. "We were hoping maybe you had some wild, embarrassing adventures when you were young."

"She said she didn't know you that well, you only had a couple of classes together," Louis added. "But she did say she barely recognized you, you've gained so much weight since then. Were you a lot skinnier when you were in school?"

Anne felt her face growing hot. "Yeah, I didn't stop with the Freshman Fifteen, I'm afraid. There used to be a lot less of me."

"So do Mary and Elizabeth take after your father, but you take after your mother?" Henry asked.

"Goodness no, our mother was thin as a rail all her life," Mary interjected. "Anne just has a bigger sweet tooth than the rest of us. That's why I keep trying to keep your mother from giving Charlie and Walter so many sweets. It's not healthy."

Anne excused herself from the room.

Alone in her room, she stared at her reflection, watching the tears as they traveled one by one down her face, and dripped off her jaw, playing the words over and over again in her head. "She barely recognized you, you've gained so much weight since then."

The gradual move from one size up to the next had never bothered her. She hadn't cared about her appearance. Her father and sister had pestered her, tried to nag, shame, and cajole her into joining them with their godawful weightlifting classes at the gym. The more they criticized her, the less she cared.

Now, for the first time in eight years, she really looked at herself in the mirror. And she didn't like what she saw.

It wasn't the weight, and her appearance. It was what the weight stood for. Back when she fell in love with Freddie, she had liked herself. She was fine with her appearance, even though she didn't obsess over it the way that her father and Elizabeth did. But she also used to take better care of herself. In college she used to swim at the pool on campus three times a week, and she would take her homework to the fitness center and ride the exercise bike while she read. She never pushed herself hard; her asthma didn't like it if she tried to push too much, but it was still good exercise. She took yoga classes, and used to love her flexibility and at the same time the endless series of challenges. There was always another thing to try for better balance, more flexibility.

When she and Freddie were together, they would both eat salads at lunch together in the cafeteria. Now, if she was honest with herself, she hardly ate anything green. She'd stopped caring after that awful day when Freddie had walked away from her.

She looked in the mirror at the result of eight years of self-neglect and self-hatred, and she didn't like what she saw. She wished Freddie could have looked at her and seen that she had improved over the years. It didn't even need to be about her physical appearance. If she would have had three Master's Degrees and a PhD to her name, or a Pulitzer Prize, or an Oscar for Best Screenplay, or a byline in The New Yorker, that would have been something. But she had nothing to show for all the intervening years.

She wondered if Freddie had said the words out of spite, calculating that Henry and Louis would repeat them to her, or if they were merely said honestly, not thinking that they might get repeated back to her. She could only assume that Freddie expected the hurtful words to reach her ears. Freddie had not forgiven her.

Well, could she blame her? Her feebleness of character, her inability to stand by her loved one in the face of adversity, wasn't something Freddie would respect. Being in a relationship with a soldier in military service took dedication and courage, not weakness and timidity. Anne couldn't blame her for being hurt, even disgusted. She was not worthy of the love Freddie had offered her.

The eyes that looked back at her in the mirror confirmed what she already knew. She was going to have to change. It was too late with Freddie, but she needed to be a person she could respect. She wanted her self-respect back.

CHAPTER 11

The problem of living at her sister and brother-in-law's house was that Anne had little control of what foods came into the house. But she did have control over what she ate. The sweets that Mary denied having in the house were everywhere: a bowl of Starburst in the living room, a bowl of chocolates in the dining room, a cookie jar full of cookies on the kitchen counter. A couple of containers of ice cream always lived in the freezer. Anne had to ignore them all, sternly and frequently repeating to herself, "She barely recognized you." The phrase always helped strengthen her resolve.

One place where she was able to exercise some control over her environment was at the dry cleaners. There was always a candy dish full of chocolates on the counter by the cash register, and there was a large bag for refilling it in the cabinet underneath. She almost threw the bag out, deciding she would treat sugar the way a smoker treats tobacco. She was going to quit cold turkey, and suffer through the withdrawal. But when a mother walked in with four children, she simply gave the entire large bag to the eldest child for her to share with her siblings.

Her family had always teased her for her fierce loyalty to Coke over Pepsi. She tried Diet Coke, but that failed to elicit anything but disgust from her taste buds. Coke Zero was better. But since she was looking to change her eating habits, she decided to give up soda altogether and stick with tea, with an occasional foray into coffee. With enough skim milk and Splenda, it wasn't too bad.

It was ironic timing that now that her father was not there with his family gym membership, she wanted to use a gym. She needed to get more exercise. It seemed a little pointless signing up for her own membership, when she wasn't going to be in New York much longer and no doubt her father already had a family membership waiting for her in Ohio. At least for now, she could still change her habits drastically by going for walks.

New York was full of public green spaces: Prospect Park close to the

Musgrove house, Green-Wood Cemetery near the dry cleaners, and of course Central Park in Manhattan.

She had gone to see an exhibit at the Metropolitan Museum of Art, and then went for a long walk on the endlessly winding trails, when she happened upon Henry and Louis walking with Freddie.

"Anne!" Henry exclaimed. "What on earth are you doing, walking alone in Central Park?"

Anne gave them a nonchalant shrug. "What does it look like I'm doing? I'm walking alone in Central Park."

Louis took her arm. "You idiot! Well, you're going to have to stick with us." He gestured at Freddie. "Have you met Anne? She's our brother's wife's sister."

"We met at your brother's house, and we already ascertained that we went to Cornell at the same time," Freddie nodded civilly to Anne.

"Hello," Anne answered her nod with a weak smile.

"We're asking for details about Freddie's glamorous career as a pilot. She's frustratingly close-mouthed about everything," Henry complained.

"Well, you know military personnel can't say much about what they're doing. Why are you asking?" Anne chastised the both of them. Her eyes met Freddie's for a moment, and Anne's voice dried up and withered away to nothing. She remembered when she was the one asking Freddie the questions about ROTC training, and Freddie would answer her with a laugh, "Well, I could tell you, but then I'd have to kill you."

"Well, what I can tell you is that the recruiters really aren't lying when they say 'It's not just a job, it's an adventure,' " Freddie offered.

Anne pretended to laugh with everyone at her quip, wishing with all her heart for a way out of their company. It was early enough in the evening; there were plenty of people about. She wasn't in any danger. Looking around, she realized that the Crofts were walking on one of the parallel paths above them. "Look, Captain Wentworth, there's your sister!"

The more people there were, the less likely it was that Freddie would be spending any time looking at her. She hoped Freddie would invite the two to join them on their walk.

"Sophie! Adam! Over here!" Freddie waved. The Crofts waved back, and came down to join them.

"What are the lot of you doing up here?" Adam asked them when they'd met and exchanged hugs and handshakes.

"Telling stories about a life of service," Freddie told them. "It's not for the faint of heart. You should tell stories about when you were chasing all over the world at Air Force bases, moving every two years. I don't know how people with families do it."

"We take care of our own quite well, I think!" Adam exclaimed stoutly. "We have some of the best schools in the nation on military bases; we want the children of military parents to have as normal an American upbringing as possible. They even have proms and football teams in high school. It's a perfectly comfortable way to grow up."

"Says someone without kids!" Freddie laughed. "The moving every few years is hard on everyone. Your spouse's career suffers, and it's not good for kids to keep getting dragged in and out of schools and unable to make friends. Even if they are American schools, there's still no stability."

"That simply doesn't matter!" Sophie Croft protested. "If you've got stability inside the family, the children are going to be fine. By the time you and the second wife came along, our father had stopped moving around so much. When I was little, we moved all the time. I just thought it was a grand adventure. I still remember my mother coming home one day, looking around, and saying, 'The house is dirty. Let's move.' I agreed with her."

"Ah, so that's why you were so ready to marry me," Adam put his arm around his wife and squeezed her waist. "You liked the gypsy nomad adventure lifestyle."

Sophie kissed him. "You mean Romany, dear. Not gypsy."

He smiled down at her. "Whatever you call the nomadic people with colorful wagons who tend to be great musicians, whom people liked to accuse of being horse thieves and children stealers. Romanticized in books, on stages and screens."

Freddie shook her head. "Well, I know all the branches try to take care of us who serve, but I still say it's hard on the families."

Sophie gave her a penetrating look. "So that's why you're still single? I'm sure you can find someone who will be more than willing to take the risk to be married to you, even if you are a career officer."

"I'd take the risk," Henry offered with a big, overblown gallant bow.

"So would I!" Louis tried to one-up his brother by taking Freddie's hand and kissing the back of it while he bowed over it.

"There, you see!" Adam concluded the discussion. "Plenty of fish in the sea. Although you're not in the navy, so we should probably say, what, plenty of birds in the sky?"

Anne watched the exchange with interest. So, Adam and Sophie didn't know Freddie's preferences. She watched Freddie's face. Was Freddie still queer, or did she change because of social pressures? Or maybe she chalked up their romantic escapade to youthful experimentation.

Freddie was laughing at Adam's expression. "You know pilots don't like birds. Especially large ones that end up on windshields or sucked into engines."

Sophie shrugged easily. "You know what he means. When you're married and have a couple kids of your own, you'll be very glad they can live on base, close to where you're stationed."

Freddie held up both her hands in a gesture of surrender. "That's it, I'm done. When the married people start talking about you'll-feel-different-when-you're-married, it's all over. I can say 'no,' and you'll say 'yes,' back and forth, over and over, and it isn't a conversation anymore. So I give up."

Anne wanted to hear more about the Crofts' adventures, remembering her own wish to follow Freddie to Germany. "How many places have you lived?" she asked them.

"Since we got married and I started dragging her around the globe with me?" Adam asked. "I won't count the places I'd been to before we were married. Let's see, we got married after I got home from the Gulf. So, that's California, Nevada, Florida, Virginia, Texas, Turkey, Italy, Germany, Norway...am I missing any?"

"Missouri, Colorado, and Japan," Sophie supplied.

Even Freddie looked in surprise at her sister while everyone made exclamations of astonishment. "Wow," Louis whistled. "The recruiters really mean it when they say you get to travel the world."

"I enjoyed seeing new places every couple of years," Sophie smiled. "I love knowing that living in Japan is not like living in Norway, and even living in Texas or Florida is not like living in California or Virginia. We always managed to find a place to live off base, so we got to know more about the places where he was stationed."

"Was it hard, living in all those places that didn't speak English?" Anne asked.

"A little, but that was part of the fun." When Sophie smiled, Anne could see that Freddie and Sophie shared the same father. It really was the same smile. "We had a sweet little apartment in Japan with a view of the ocean that I still miss, and a sushi restaurant between the train stop and the apartment that was fabulous. The hiking in Norway was breathtaking, and the sweaters I bought there are so thick and warm, I can survive the worst winters in New York without a shiver."

"Did you ever find yourself in a strange place, by yourself, while Adam was deployed and you couldn't join him?"

"I was in Turkey while Adam was in Iraq," Sophie remembered soberly. "I would characterize that time as the most stressful years of my life." She looked fondly up at her husband. "I knew what kind of a daredevil he was, so I could only assume he was doing something risky, and stupid, and heroic. Imagination can be a terrible thing to have as a military spouse. But I kept myself occupied. I learned a lot of the Turkish language, and Turkish cooking, and the time passed. Eventually he came home to me, safe and sound."

"I knew I'd be in more trouble with my wife than with my commanding officer, if I failed to come home," Adam Croft concluded with an adoring look back into his wife's face.

Having stood for so long where they had come upon each other, the party picked a direction to continue their walk in Central Park. Being six in number meant that some of the time they walked in two groups of three, and some of the time they walked in three groups of two. But Anne and Freddie always managed to never be paired together.

At one point, Anne was able to hear past the Crofts to the conversation the Musgrove boys were having with Freddie. "Anne? No, we've all kind of given up on her. We thought maybe she was thinking of graduate school for a while, but I don't think she got into the program that she wanted. We have no idea what she's looking for in a guy. We don't really know what kind of life plans she has. But we're glad she's here, we always like it when she comes around."

When they finished their walk and said their goodbyes, she was painfully aware of the way they both avoided eye contact with each other. The cold politeness when Freddie said goodbye to her in front of their families was the most miserable moment of Anne's already rather miserable life.

CHAPTER 12

When Freddie's training class got postponed, and then postponed again, she elected to use up more of her accumulated leave to spend her unoccupied time in New York, instead of cooling her heels at the base in New Jersey. Anne learned the news that she was still in the city from Henry and Louis, gleefully reading aloud their text conversations.

"And I must say I'm not the least bit sorry," Louis read aloud from his phone, "if it means more time to hang out with you guys. There's no better way to see New York City than with a native guide!"

"We're going to go see Spamalot tonight!" Henry told them enthusiastically. "Freddie went to the TKTS line as soon as it opened up, and got us three seats together!" His phone chirped in his hand, which Anne had learned meant that he was getting a text. He looked down at his phone, and then rolled his eyes in annoyance. "It's Charlotte Hayter again."

Charles looked up from the couch, where he had been mostly ignoring the conversation while watching ESPN with the sound turned off. "How is your girlfriend? You haven't seen much of her lately, have you?"

"She's not my girlfriend," Henry corrected him. "We just hang out together a lot."

"What's the difference?" Charles asked.

"It's…different," Henry struggled to explain. "Mom and Mrs. Hayter are best friends, so we grew up together. We hang out sometimes. We couldn't date, that would be weird. Like dating your sister, or something."

"Does she know that?" Charles asked.

"Of course she does," Mary interjected into the conversation. "Charles, you don't understand how things are these days. It's…complicated."

Charles smirked at Henry. "I don't know, the way she looks at you, I definitely think there are…complications."

Henry rolled his eyes. "You're imagining things."

Louis was impatiently handing Henry his jacket. "We don't have time to explain the dating scene to old people right now, if we don't get moving

A Woman's Persuasion

we'll be late meeting up with Freddie! Let's move!"

The boys left with a happy wave, leaving Mary and Charles to continue what was obviously an old argument.

"Freddie obviously prefers Henry," Mary insisted as soon as the door had closed.

"Well, I think she prefers Louis," Charles changed channels on the television, looking to see what other games were on. "But quite frankly, it would be a great thing for either one of the boys if they can snag her."

"How much money does a fighter pilot make in the Air Force?" Mary asked, with a grin that looked perfectly avaricious to Anne. It would have been comical, if it wasn't such a completely uncomfortable conversation to be witnessing.

"I'm sure the money must be terrific," Charles settled on basketball.

"I wonder what sort of promotions they get," Mary gleefully continued her speculations. "Are there admirals in the Air Force, or generals?"

"I think there are, but there are a few ranks she would have to gain before becoming a general," Charles was losing interest in the conversation in direct proportion to his interest in the game he was watching. "Aw, how can you miss a free throw like that?"

"After Captain, it's Major, then Lieutenant Colonel, then Colonel, then Brigadier General, I believe," Anne volunteered, then immediately wished she hadn't.

"How do you know that?" Mary asked. "That can't be right."

"I'm probably not, but I had a friend in the Air Force in college," Anne shrugged nonchalantly, and tried not to blush. When she could feel her face growing warm, she made a show of bending down to pick up toys off the floor and returning them to the boys' toy box.

"Well, I hope there are titles for the people married to people in the Air Force," Mary concluded. "A title would look good on Henry."

"Titles don't work that way, outside of British royalty in those romance novels you like to read." Charles never took his eyes off the television. "You have to earn them in the military, you don't marry them."

"Well, Henry would still look good as a military spouse for all those balls and ceremonies," Mary persisted. "You have to admit, he's better-looking than Louis."

Charles stopped watching the game and looked at his wife. "You just want it to be Henry that Freddie likes, instead of Louis, to break him up with Charlotte."

Mary's shoulder twitched. "Well, I'm sure your mother and Mrs. Hayter have been dreaming of having the two of them get married since they were born weeks apart, but really. Half black and half Puerto Rican? The babies would all end up with that impossible frizzy black hair."

"Who cares what kind of hair the children would have?" Charles looked mystified. "Maybe neither of them even wants kids."

"Well, I can only hope Henry means it when he says he's not interested in Charlotte," Mary sighed. "Because I completely agree with you, Charles. The way Charlotte looks at him, she's definitely interested in him."

Charles' pager went off, and he checked the number. "Ah, the security system is down again at the Greenpoint store. I need to call in and see if I need to go over there. But you know, I hope Henry does end up with Charlotte. She's a sweet girl, she's clearly nuts about him, he could do a whole hell of a lot worse. And I happen to like her hair. She's got beautiful curls."

As soon as Charles had left the room, Mary turned to Anne. "I don't care what Charles thinks, I think it would be something awful for Henry to marry Charlotte. People should stick to their own kind. But it's a moot point, I'm sure Freddie likes Henry better. I wish you could have been here when they were both reading their texts out loud. Freddie clearly is flirting with Henry, and just being friendly with Louis. You would have thought so, too, if you could have heard it."

Anne made a noncommittal noise, and left the room.

A few days after that conversation, which had managed to be unpleasant in more ways all at once than Anne would have thought possible, Anne found herself in an even more awkward and unpleasant situation.

She and the boys were alone at the dry cleaning shop, while Mary went to a doctor's appointment. She was expecting Henry and Louis to come by to pick up Charlie and Walter, so that she wouldn't have to try to close up shop while also trying to manage the boys. Charlie was much less rambunctious while he was still recovering from his injury, but it made him restless and whiny, not necessarily any more quiet. Walter was picking up the slack where his brother had left off, and was becoming a seemingly bigger handful with every passing day.

Walter was on the floor occupied by a fleet of toy trucks. Charlie was sitting on the couch in the corner Mary had brought into the store to create a little corner where the children – or customers, for that matter – could sit. Anne was sitting with him, reading to him, when the buzzer sounded, announcing a customer opening the door. She looked up, expecting the Musgrove boys, and her voice died away at the sight of Freddie Wentworth standing there.

The two of them stared at each other for a moment, until Charlie insisted that Anne continue reading to him.

"Not until we say hello to Captain Wentworth, and find out why she is gracing us with her presence today," Anne put the book down. "Why don't you go say hello?"

Charlie slid off the couch, sauntered over to Freddie, and started singing to her. "I love you, you love me, we're a happy family," he warbled with an amusingly serious face.

Anne didn't think there was a single adult in the United States that liked the Barney song. Her eyes met Freddie's apologetically. "Both the boys love Barney. I have not been able to figure out the fascination, but he seems to be surprisingly popular among everyone under 6 years old."

"There must be something reassuring about large purple fuzzy creatures. McDonalds used to have Grimace, I'm sure they were marketing to the same audience," Freddie responded. She looked around the store. "Are Henry and Louis here? They told me to meet them here."

"I'm expecting them any time now," she answered. She would have said more, but the buzzer sounded again, this time admitting Charlotte Hayter. "Why, hello Charlotte! This is a pleasant surprise!"

"Hello, Anne. I heard you were going to come fill in while Jane was on maternity leave. I assume you've seen Henry?" she handed over her claim ticket for her dry cleaning.

"He should be getting here any time now," Freddie told her. "He and Louis are both coming here to collect their nephews."

"And who are you?" Charlotte asked.

"I'm Freddie Wentworth."

"You're Captain Wentworth?" Charlotte asked. "I thought you were a man."

Anne disappeared to go find Charlotte's dry cleaning.

The two women were not talking, just eying each other warily when she got back. "Here you go, Charlotte. Looks like you prepaid, so you're all set."

She had walked around in front of the counter to hand over the dry cleaning bags, which included some sort of long garment like a coat. "Just put that on the hook for a second, so I can put my purse in my backpack," Charlotte told her.

Anne complied, and was glad when Charlie offered a distraction by coming over to her and demanding that she tie his shoe for him.

While she was kneeling in front of him, Walter, jealous that his brother was getting more attention than him, came up behind Anne and threw himself onto her back. Surprised, Anne toppled over onto the ground in a most undignified position.

"Walter! That was uncalled for. Get off of me, I need my other hand to get up. I think I hurt my wrist," Anne scolded. She tried to peel his arms off of her, but her one hand was pinned awkwardly by his grip, and the other hand hurt when she tried to close her hand around the little arm. "Let go of me right now, Walter."

"Shame on you, Walter, you should do as you're told," Charlotte scolded him. "Why don't you come over here to your Aunt Charlotte," she cajoled.

The little arms squeezed all the more stubbornly around Anne, and then she realized he was shifting his weight, and trying to climb her. She was in the process of deciding her next move, when suddenly the little miscreant was no longer clinging to her.

It was Freddie who had come to her rescue. She had plucked him off of Anne, and was sitting him on the couch with a talk about how important it was to listen to his commanding officer.

Anne stood up slowly, examining her wrist and listening to her own heart thudding loudly in her ears. She didn't think there was any serious damage, she had just fallen on it awkwardly. She shook out her hand and listened to Freddie's continued conversation with Walter. Freddie was completely absorbed in the child, and absolutely would not meet her eyes. The kindness of the rescue, and at the same time the cold shoulder she was getting, confused her. All she could assume was that Freddie did not want Anne's silent thanks, and had only come to Anne's rescue because Freddie did not like poorly disciplined children.

She gnawed on her lower lip, still kneading her wrist. Charlie stood next to her, watching with some awe as his little brother was getting lectured by the formidable woman who was a captain and a pilot. Charlotte also watched the same conversation, frowning, saying nothing. Somehow through the silence Anne felt that Charlotte was annoyed that Freddie had come to Anne's rescue, instead of herself.

Anne was relieved when the buzzer sounded and this time, Henry and Louis entered. Henry was clearly startled to see Charlotte in the shop. "What are you doing here?" he asked in a voice that was less than friendly.

"Picking up my dry cleaning. You ever going to answer any of my texts?" Charlotte's voice matched his in coolness.

"I've been busy. I'll catch up with you when I can." Henry looked from Louis, who was now holding Walter, to Freddie, who had taken hold of Charlie's hand. "You guys ready? Let's get going."

Soon the buzzer sounded with the departure of all parties, leaving Anne alone to bury her face among the dry cleaning bags. The plastic felt cool against her cheeks.

CHAPTER 13

The dry cleaners closed for Thanksgiving weekend, and Anne was enjoying the time off. Ever since Freddie's visit, the store ceased being a place of refuge where she could lose herself in thoughts of schedules, sales receipts, and supplies. Every time she helped a client at the counter, she saw Freddie's statuesque figure coming in the door. If she sat on the little couch, she saw Freddie sitting there, studiously scolding Walter.

Mary, however, seemed less content to be home on Saturday. Charles had an extra ticket to the Giants game and asked Freddie to go with him, and so he was gone most of the afternoon. Even though she was not a sports fan, Mary was put out that she had not been invited, and paced restlessly, fidgeting with knick knacks and picture frames. She rushed to the door when she heard Henry and Louis on the stairs. "Where are you boys off to?"

"Hey, Mary!" Louis was still putting on a heavy hooded sweatshirt while he talked. "Henry and I are going out to the botanical gardens. The Christmas lights are up, and they've got half price admission this weekend for students with ID. See you later, we won't be around for dinner."

"Wait!" Mary cried. "I want to come with you! Just give me a minute to get the boys up from their naps, and we'll come, too."

Louis and Henry exchanged a look. "Well, it's an hour on the subway to get out there," Henry cautioned.

"Of course it's an hour on the subway, it's all the way out in the Bronx," Mary was pulling out the stroller.

"It's going to take a long time to get there, and then once we get there it's a lot of walking," Louis took a turn at trying to dissuade her.

"Have I suddenly developed a phobia for riding on the subway, or something? And walking?" She handed them both the coats for the two boys. "I'll be right back with the boys, and we can leave."

Henry and Louis looked mournfully at her departing back, and then imploringly at Anne. "By the time she gets them up and dressed, and finds their bottles and snacks and diaper bags and whatever else, it's going to be another hour and a half before we get out the door," Louis said. "Can't you dissuade her from coming?"

Anne put down her book. "Probably not. She's been pacing around here like a caged animal. She's been making it impossible to read."

"Well, then, I know if we take her you can actually have some quiet and read, but would you come with us?" Henry asked. "You can handle Walter and Charlie better than anyone else, and then, too, we might not have to kill Mary by the time we're only halfway there."

Anne looked regretfully at her book, then at Henry and Louis' pleading faces as they listened to Mary coming back, fussing as she dropped shoes and sweatshirts while hustling her sleepy progeny in front of her. With a sigh, she smiled at the two Musgrove men, and turned to get the boys quickly into shoes, coats, and hats by challenging them to a race.

Even with Anne's expert handling, it still took almost half an hour to get out the door and down the street to the subway station. As they were approaching, who should happen to be coming out but Charles and Freddie.

"Well, hello!" Louis exclaimed enthusiastically at the sight of Freddie, all impatience at the long delay in getting started forgotten. "How was the game?"

"It was great!" Charles launched into what was obviously going to be a long and detailed description, but Henry interrupted him.

"We're going to the botanical gardens to see the Christmas lights," he informed them, but his eyes were only for Freddie. "You want to come along?"

"You can tell us about the game while we're on the subway," Louis added, seeing Charles' hurt expression at being ignored.

Charles brightened back up with the invitation. "Sure, I'm game! Freddie?"

Freddie was laughing. "Far be it from me to pass up another outing in New York with native guides! Let's do it!"

Being such a large group meant conversations on the subway were sporadic and disjointed as people crowded on and cleared off the train. Henry and Louis asked Freddie questions about the game, which Charles answered. Mary told Charles that both boys were outgrowing their clothes and they needed to go shopping. Freddie told Mary that she was glad that Charlie seemed to be recovering well after his tumble. Charlie, having been impressed by Freddie's authority the other day, was telling Freddie that he was going to be a captain in the Air Force, too.

"You're going to be an Air Force pilot when you grow up?" Mary asked her son.

"Not when I grow up, next week," Charlie corrected her.

The most difficult conversation to overhear happened just before the train reached their stop. Louis and Freddie were standing immediately behind Anne, where she was squashed between three teenaged girls and a tired-looking heavy-set man in a rumpled business suit. Louis asked Freddie what her sister was doing today.

"Oh, Adam has talked her into going ice skating at Rockefeller Center. She's not particularly coordinated, and will probably spend more time on her ass than on her skates," Freddie shook her head at her sister's lack of grace. "But Adam loves to be active, and she is infinitely willing to try anything. I do wish she had a little more sense of self-preservation. She managed to break her leg trying to learn to ski, ended up in the emergency room after taking a bad spill on a 3-day bicycle trip, and broke her arm falling off a horse. But no matter what crazy thing Adam comes up with, she's willing to go off and try it."

"Well, of course she is," Louis exclaimed. "It's so obvious that they're nuts about each other. There was no missing the fact at that reception we got to go to at Anne's old place. If I loved a woman as much as Adam loves your sister, and she had as adventurous a spirit as your sister, I would do everything I can to facilitate her. There are people who like to squash an adventurous soul. Like the wives who don't want their husbands becoming astronauts. But life is risk, and I'd rather take risks together, than live a boring life of security."

"Hear, hear!" Freddie exclaimed.

No more was said for a few moments, and then they were all moving toward the doors, onto the platform, and making their way into the park.

The pleasure of arriving at their destination was rather dulled for Anne. She trudged behind the group, trying not to compare Louis' last statement to her own life and life choices, despising herself more and more with each passing moment. She paid for her park admission, and looked over Charles' shoulder at the park map he had unfolded in front of him. She saw the list of buildings on the grounds. "Does Mrs. Hayter still work at the gift shop here on weekends?" she asked no one in particular.

Since she had asked no one, no one answered her. She assumed nobody had heard her, since there were several opinions floating through the air about which direction to take.

At Mary's insistence, they headed toward the children's adventure garden, and Santa's house. The path they walked took them straight to the reflecting pool, which was just down the lane from the gift shop, cafeterias, and the information booth.

"Hey," Charles exclaimed, "let's go see if Mrs. Hayter is working today! We should say hello. And if she's not in, we can leave a message on her desk or something."

Mary was not eager to make any such visit. "We shouldn't bother her while she's working. That would be rude."

"We're saying hello, we're not going to sit down and stay for tea," Charles argued. "There's nothing rude about saying hello."

"Well, I think it would be rude, and I'm not going to do it," Mary answered stoutly.

No one in the group was fooled by Mary's rationale for not paying the visit. "Well, I'm going to go. Who's joining me?"

"Well, Anne won't. She's got manners and knows better. Besides, I need her help with the strollers." Mary dug her fingers into Anne's arm, and started pulling her in the other direction. Anne looked at Henry, to see if perhaps he would come to her rescue, rather than face the awkward situation of facing Charlotte Hayter's mother. But the rest of the party was walking toward the library building. As Anne watched their retreating backs, she caught Freddie throwing a contemptuous glance over her shoulder. Anne knew how Freddie despised racism and racists, and hoped the glance was aimed only at Mary, not at the both of them.

Instead of heading to the children's garden, Mary took Anne and the boys in the other direction. Soon they were standing in front of the grand old Victorian wintergarden, outlined beautifully in white lights. But rather than going inside, Mary insisted they ought to turn back to see if Charles was done with his visit. As they turned back, Louis and Freddie were approaching.

"Were you not successful in finding Mrs. Hayter?" Anne asked, while Mary studiously looked away.

"Oh, we found her," Louis reported. "And what do you think? Charlotte also happens to be here! She came here to bring her mother some lunch, and got drafted into doing some volunteer work. So Charles and Henry are both tied up in conversation. We got bored listening to Charles tell the story of the Giants game all over again, so we made our escape. We didn't pay admission to stand around listening to Charles talk." With that, Louis and Freddie wandered away to admire the giant Christmas tree that was installed across from the grand conservatory.

By now, Charlie's young bladder had all it could take, and the little boy announced that he needed the bathroom. Anne volunteered to take charge of the situation while Mary waited for Charles and Henry to re-emerge. After taking care of the problem at the bathroom in the conservatory, Anne did not feel like hurrying back to join her sister, and stopped to explain various plants and leaves to Charlie. Fortunately, he was surprisingly interested in her explanations of bromeliads.

She was crouched down, pointing out some fine specimens to her nephew, when Louis' voice floated through the densely-growing plants.

"Charlotte's really a great gal, and never mind all of Henry's protests that he's not interested, and she's too much like a sister to us. I don't believe all that rot for a minute. He likes her. Maybe he's not as nuts about her as she is about him, but that's because he's stupid. I love my brother, but let's face it, he's stupid."

"Spoken like a good brother," Anne heard the amusement in Freddie's voice.

"Well, if I'm a good brother I'll convince him to ask her out. She's smart, she's funny, she's stable, and she's only crazy in a good way. He could do a whole lot worse. Hell, she's even got a raunchy sense of humor, so she's probably good in bed. So what's not to like?"

"Well, if you all grew up together, why haven't you asked her out?" Freddie asked.

"I thought about it for a long time, but she's really got the hots for Henry, not me. And frankly, they are more perfect together. They both like puzzles, and horror movies, and rain. I have no patience for puzzles, I don't like horror movies, and I hate rain. Call me a romantic, but it's nice to have those sorts of connections inside a relationship."

"You really are a romantic, aren't you," Freddie exclaimed. "And, wow, speaking of romantic, look at these. They are almost exactly the same color as your eyes."

Anne missed whatever was said next, when Charlie had questions about the display in front of them. She answered absently, wanting to escape, and yet not wanting to leave when the little boy was genuinely interested in the floral displays. She was about to ask Charlie if he would like to leave when more snippets of conversation held her rooted to the spot.

"Ah, Mary isn't all bad," Louis was saying. "She pulls her weight at home, and Charles says she really does help with the dry cleaning business. But as you've seen, her attitudes belong in a different century. I almost expected her to call Mrs. Hayter a darkie or use the 'N' word. Some of her other politics aren't much better. We all wish that Charles had married Anne instead. Did you know he dated Anne before he met Mary?"

"Really?" Anne tried to read what Freddie was thinking from her voice, but she had no success with nothing to go on but one word.

"Really. Anne's the one who introduced them. I don't know why she didn't keep dating Charles, I think she liked him well enough. About all I could guess is that Anne doesn't like sports much. Not that Mary is much about them either, but I guess she likes a football game better than Anne does. Anne is a bit more cerebral than Charles, but we like to think that she could have made it work. She and Charles are both such good-natured people, we all think they would have been great together."

The voices got fainter, and Charlie was ready to give up on plants and get back to doing some running. Anne was glad to go back into the brisk late November air; she needed the cold air on her cheeks.

There was a cheerful tunnel of lights between the gift shop and the conservatory where everyone gradually congregated. Anne was surprised and amused to see Charlotte Hayter join the group while holding hands with Henry. So it would seem Henry had removed himself from his contest with his brother for Freddie's attention.

But was Freddie interested in changing teams? Did Louis have a chance?

Anne had plenty of opportunities to watch and wonder as the group meandered from one light display to the next, and from one botanical display to the next. Freddie spent plenty of time with Louis, laughed at his jokes, smiled as she examined the beauty around her. But then, she also laughed at Henry's jokes, and Charles' jokes. Even Charlotte made an attempt to give up her rivalry with Freddie, and the two women put their heads close together to read a sign. For all Anne knew, Freddie was interested in Charlotte.

Walter and Charlie collectively put an end to Anne's surreptitious scrutiny of Freddie. Walter managed to wriggle out from the confines of his stroller, and took off across the lawn in between the rows of tulip trees. Charlie was the first to realize his brother had escaped, and soon took off after him. Perhaps to capture his brother, perhaps to simply join him in his escape. Either way, they both had a significant head start when Anne realized they had taken off on their own, and dashed off to catch them.

She was just trying to decide what she was going to do when she reached her nephews, when her foot caught on something, and she toppled to the ground. Charlie was immediately in front of her, and somehow she managed to catch him in her arms so she did not fall on top of him, and turned so that her shoulder and arm took the majority of the impact.

She heard the Musgroves behind her gasp collectively at her fall. Behind her, Charles had scooped up Walter, and came over to help her off the ground, while Charlie tried to help, too. "That was a most impressive tackle, Anne! I had no idea you were such a good football player."

Anne did not take his offered hand, and got on her hands and knees for a moment before standing up. She was feeling a little queasy from the hard landing, and now her shoulder and arm were really aching. "I didn't know I was, either."

They wandered back over to the rest of the group. Anne felt slow and stupid, sprawling ungracefully on the ground in front of everyone. When they all looked at her with concern, it only reinforced the fact that absolutely everyone had seen her clumsy performance. And here she'd been feeling like she was making progress, taking longer walks and getting a temporary gym membership so she could start swimming and taking yoga again.

The group had barely started the trek back toward the subway stop, when Freddie paused in surprise. "Sophie? Adam?"

Indeed, the Crofts were bearing down upon them. There was a great exchange of hugs and exclamations and chastisements, since neither sister had thought to call the other to say she was going to see the Christmas lights at the botanical garden.

"I thought you were going skating," Freddie said.

"We did, but that was this morning," Sophie laughed. "You didn't think I'd do that all day, did you?"

Freddie shrugged ruefully.

"We were just heading back to the car," Adam told her. "I'd offer you a ride, but we're not actually going home. We're going straight from here to a party in Brooklyn."

"Well, if you're going to Brooklyn, could I prevail upon you to make an extra stop on your way to your party? Anne took a nasty spill. It would be much easier on her to ride home in a car, instead of standing on crowded subways for an hour." Freddie didn't even look at Anne as she made the request of her sister.

The mortification of her fall hit Anne all over again. "Oh, I'll be fine," she demurred.

"Nonsense!" Sophie insisted. "We'd be happy to take you home."

Before Anne had a chance to protest, Freddie had given her a gentle nudge, and she was walking away with the Crofts, while the rest of the group was heading back to the subway station.

She didn't realize she'd been cradling her elbow until the Crofts paused outside the first aid station. "Let's stop in and get them to take a look at your arm. At least they can give you a band-aid or an ice pack, whichever seems more necessary."

Anne would have protested that she was fine, but she gave in to their concern and the rather unpleasant throbbing of her arm. The EMT looked her over, declared there should be nothing more to worry about than some bruises, and sent her away with a cold pack.

Adam Croft insisted on running ahead, and he was waiting at the curb for them when they emerged from the park. "Door to door service," he announced cheerfully, jumping out of the car to hold the door open for Anne.

When everyone was settled, Adam steered the car out of the parking lot, out of the park and onto the Bronx River Parkway. "So, Anne, maybe you can lend us some insight. Has either Henry or Louis asked Freddie out yet?"

"It seems like they're inviting her to stuff all the time. Except on days like today, when my brother-in-law beat them to it," Anne answered, knowing that was not what he was asking.

"No, I mean have either Henry or Louis asked Freddie out? Like, on a date?" Adam persisted.

"Not that I know of," Anne answered slowly.

"Well, I wish they'd get on with it already!" Sophie exclaimed. "Freddie's training class starts Monday, and so we'll be seeing less of her, and then when she's done, she'll be gone."

"Maybe that's why they're holding off," Anne speculated. "Starting a relationship and immediately have it turn into a long distance relationship isn't very sensible."

"Meh. We were a long distance relationship when we first met," Adam told her. Sophie continued for him, "And then we got married. You're such a prudent person, Anne, you would be horrified to know how we got engaged and married when we hardly knew each other."

"So, horrify me," Anne offered. She would rather hear them tell the story of how they met and married than listen to them speculate about Freddie all the way to Brooklyn.

CHAPTER 14

"I don't suppose the lot of you would be interested in taking a trip with me up to Rhode Island, now that both Louis and Henry are done with their finals?" Freddie said by way of hello, stepping into the Musgrove's front room a couple of Fridays later.

Henry and Louis brightened, as always, at the sight of Freddie. "Really? Why Rhode Island?"

"I've just found out that a friend who served with me when we were stationed on the *Laconia* is living in Newport," Freddie explained. "It's about 6 hours by train from here. I don't suppose some of you would like to go spend this weekend checking out Newport? It's supposed to be a neat place. Full of old mansions and a harbor town. Very New England, from what Captain Harville tells me."

"Captain Harville? Is that your friend?" Henry asked eagerly. Anne noticed that, despite his holding hands with Charlotte at the botanical garden, he was no less enamored of Freddie than he was before.

"Yes. George Harville. He and his wife Amanda apparently moved to Rhode Island after he got injured in a plane crash."

Louis' eyes were big as saucers. "It's possible to survive a plane crash?"

Freddie looked amused. "They invest too much money in us pilots to not give us a few safety precautions. But sometimes things go wrong. After they patched him up, they let him go. George is doing consulting work now." She looked at all the Musgroves, and Anne was included in the glance that was an invitation. "He's offered us overnight crash space, if any of you would like to go explore Newport with me for the weekend."

There was a general hubbub. Mr. and Mrs. Musgrove offered to babysit the boys, Charles agreed to leave the dry cleaners in the hands of subordinates, and they all planned to meet at Penn Station the first thing in the morning.

When they alighted at the Seastreak Ferry Terminal, a tall, dark man quietly approached behind Freddie, and the moment she turned around, he snatched her up in a bear hug.

There was much laughter, and more hugs when first a short woman with thick sideswept bangs, and then a sad-faced young woman with short dark hair also stepped forward to greet Freddie. After initial greetings were completed, Freddie introduced her old friends to her new ones.

"Captain George Harville, Mrs. Amanda Harville, Captain Jamie Benwick, I'd like you to meet the Musgroves. This is Louis, and Henry, Charles and his wife Mary, and Mary's sister Anne. Jamie had been engaged to George's brother when he died. As for the Musgroves, Mary and Anne's father sold my sister her apartment in New York."

There was a general round of pleasantries and handshakes, backpacks and other sorts of overnight bags were stowed in trunks, and the party was bundled into cars for the short ride to Bellevue Avenue and the row of mansions built by millionaires in the Gilded Age.

The Harvilles insisted on starting with Marble House. "If you see The Breakers first, everything else seems so... small," Captain Harville explained. "We have time for two this afternoon, and then we can show you The Elms tomorrow. Unfortunately, you've come during the off season, so many of the mansions are closed down."

"But the ones that are open are decorated for Christmas, and they are really spectacular to see," Amanda Harville enthused. "So I would say your timing is quite wonderful."

Marble House was nothing less than a palace. Richard Morris Hunt had built it for Alva Vanderbilt in 1892, although it sounded like Mrs. Vanderbilt would have been a perfectly fine architect in her own right, had such a career been available to women in the 1890s. The party marveled loudly at the ornate front doors, the frescoed ceilings and gilded trim of the gold salon, the ornate details of the fireplace and woodwork in the gothic room. And the Christmas decorations really were as spectacular as Amanda had promised. "We are such amateurs at interior design, nowadays," Mary exclaimed.

The Breakers was perhaps less ornate in furnishings, but was even more massive in size. The great hall in the center of the house was a 50 foot by 50 foot by 50 foot cube. Either the Vanderbilt brothers had a competitive streak, or their wives did; since Willie K had built Marble House for his wife Alva, Cornelius had to build an even bigger house for his wife Alice. Several two-story Christmas trees and hundreds of potted poinsettias emphasized the size of the space by their inability to look anything other than tiny in the huge space.

Anne found the spaces so overwhelmingly large, she stood in the corners of the rooms to try and take everything in. Captain Benwick wandered past her slowly as they were touring the music room. "In the greenest of our valleys, by good angels tenanted, once a fair and stately palace – radiant palace – reared its head," she muttered softly to herself.

Anne recognized the poem. "In the monarch Thought's dominion it stood there! Never seraph spread a pinion over fabric half so fair," she quoted the rest of the verse.

Captain Benwick looked at Anne in surprise. "I didn't think anyone else out there knew any Edgar Allen Poe that wasn't *The Telltale Heart* or *The Raven*."

Anne shrugged. "Being an English major might not lead to a career, but it does make one highly educated in things that no one cares about anymore."

Captain Benwick smiled at her. "Poetry certainly does seem to qualify as one of those things no one cares about. But ever since Frank died, I've discovered there are so many classic poets who know how to put what I'm feeling into words."

"Is that why you know Poe?" Anne realized. "Since *The Raven* is about grieving for lost love?"

"Vainly had I sought to borrow from my books surcease of sorrow – sorrow for the lost Lenore," she quoted to Anne with a sad smile.

"For the rare and radiant maiden whom the angels name Lenore, nameless here forevermore," Anne quoted back.

"You also understand loss," Captain Benwick observed soberly.

Anne could hear Freddie and Louis' laughter echoing from the next room. "Yes," she admitted soberly as they strolled into the library. "I know something about loss."

They stopped in the doorway. The library was stunning. The fireplace looked like it belonged in a medieval cathedral, and the ceiling had beautiful wooden beams with colorful painted motifs nestled between them. Like every other room they visited, it was also adorned abundantly with Christmas trees and poinsettias.

"Looks like a waffle, doesn't it," Charles said to Anne and Captain Benwick as he passed them, tilting his head back to examine the ceiling.

"The splendor falls on castle walls," Anne quoted, wondering if her companion knew Tennyson.

"And snowy summits old in story, the long light shakes across the lakes, and the wild cataract leaps in glory," Captain Benwick continued. "Blow, bugle, blow, set the wild echoes flying, blow, bugle, answer; echoes dying, dying, dying."

"Well, Captain Benwick," Anne laughed, "Poetry certainly does give expression to your feelings. So have you read any nice, cheerful prose lately? What did you think of the last Harry Potter book?"

"There was a lot of death in it," she pointed out. "And, please, call me Jamie. I'm not in the military anymore."

After The Breakers, the Harvilles took the entire party back to their house, which was a fairly humble cottage overlooking the sea. Upon arriving, the guests discovered that the Harvilles had packed off all three of their children to stay with friends, so that there was enough space for everyone to sleep. Mary and Charles had the girls' room, Freddie bunked with Jamie in their son's room, Louis and Henry had the pullout couch in the living room, and Anne had the reclining chair in the den.

The party felt guilty about crowding their hosts so badly, and wished they would have known to rent a hotel. But the Harvilles seemed cheerfully unaware of any crowding or discomfort.

Eating dinner in the cottage also made the guests feel like an imposition on their hosts. The meal was simple, but plentiful, but the plain pot roast and carrots and potatoes were bland, and most of the guests would have preferred a good clam chowder while they happened to be in Rhode Island. But even Mary had enough manners not to say so. Hard to be critical, when Amanda Harville kept gushing about how much fun it was to have a house full of guests, and how much she enjoyed breaking in her new roasting pan in honor of the arrival of Freddie and her friends.

The warmth of their hosts' hospitality threw Anne into a blue mood that did not lift the rest of the evening. "Had I not broken it off with Freddie when I did, these people would be my close friends, too," she kept thinking. "When they laugh together and retell old stories, I would be remembering with them."

It made her a poor contributor to the conversations all evening, and it made for a long time before she was finally able to fall asleep.

CHAPTER 15

Henry was the only person awake when Anne emerged, dressed, from the bathroom. They looked around the little kitchen, feeling awkward with their hosts still asleep. "Want to go find coffee?" Henry whispered to her, trying not to wake Louis still sleeping in the living room. Anne nodded her assent, and they both grabbed their coats and slipped quietly out the door.

Once outside, however, the view of the ocean from the front porch lured them down to the shore. After a few moments for admiration, they started walking to the wharf. Among the artisan's galleries and tourist shops they found a little café where they could get coffee and breakfast. Henry was surprised when Anne only ordered coffee and two eggs.

"You're passing up on anything from the bakery? But everything in the window looked amazing."

"You go ahead," Anne encouraged him. "Don't let me spoil your fun." It was the first time anyone had noticed that Anne hadn't eaten anything with sugar since the day she'd heard that Freddie hadn't even recognized her.

Once they had placed their orders and got their coffee, Henry entertained Anne with a long, enthusiastic tirade about the benefits of sea air, and listed all the people he knew with respiratory problems in New York who would benefit greatly from moving out of the city. Anne was amused that it never occurred to him that Anne herself was moving out of the city, once she was done helping Charles and Mary with the dry cleaning business. She had to be the one to point it out to him.

"I suppose that's true!" he exclaimed. "I'm sorry, it's so natural for you to be here with us. Have you heard much from your father or sister? And how about Lanie Russell? She didn't move, did she? Why hasn't she been coming out to Brooklyn to see you?"

Anne opened up her mouth to answer, but Henry started talking again before any sound came out. "You know, I wish I had the nerve to get to know her better. She's such a formidable woman. I'm actually afraid of her.

She seems like she could persuade anyone to do just about anything. She would be fearsome in a courtroom. Louis should be getting to know her even more than me; he could probably learn a thing or two about how to win arguments and influence people."

When they finished eating, paid, and went back outside, who should happen to be strolling down the street, but Freddie and Louis. Louis wanted to take advantage of the tourist district to do some Christmas shopping, and the rest of them helped window shop.

As they stepped into an interesting-looking store, a tall man was coming out. He held the door open for their party, and Anne blushed when she realized he was checking her out. Her hair was blown about from the ocean breezes, her cheeks were pink, and she had been laughing at the banter going on between Henry and Louis. She knew Freddie was the intended audience, but they were being particularly witty. She smiled up at the stranger to thank him for holding the door for them, and was surprised by the interest in his face as she passed him.

The four of them wandered around the store for some time, admiring this, exclaiming over that. But the price tags were frequently beyond Louis' budget. Eventually, he settled upon a shot glass for his father, and a scarf for his mother. Anne was deciding if she wanted to buy the silver necklace and earring set that looked like little anchors, while Louis was completing his purchase. Henry was standing at the door, watching the street. "There's Charles and Mary! I'll go catch them!" He dashed out the door.

Anne decided against the anchor jewelry and hurried out the door after the rest of her party, just in time to be nearly run over by the same gentleman who had held the door open earlier.

He had a hand on each of her arms. "I'm so sorry. Are you all right?" he asked hastily, looking down at her with genuine concern.

"The only thing hurt is my pride, I should know how to look where I'm going," Anne answered ruefully.

"Well, good, as long as you're okay. I'm in a bit of a rush," the man said. He gave her arm one last pat, then resumed his dash. Anne's companions watched with her in surprise as he jumped into a waiting limosine, which then sped away.

"Damned pretentious jerk," a woman next to Mary on the sidewalk muttered, staring after the limo.

"You know him?" Mary asked her.

"Yeah, that's William Elliot," the stranger told Mary. "He's a big financier from New York. He married into one of the richest families in Newport. You're obviously not from around here, or you'd know his face from all the press coverage."

"No, we're from the city, too," Mary explained.

"New York," Freddie elaborated with a smile. "People from Manhattan forget there are any other cities besides New York."

"Well, he married Andrea Nelson. Heir to all the Nelson family money. It was all over the local news. You couldn't buy groceries or get a cup of coffee without hearing about it. Then a couple of years later, she's dead. He's out there flaunting her money, and can barely bother to look like he's honestly even grieving for her. A lot of people around here wonder if he killed her."

"William Elliot. That's not a relation of ours, is it?" Mary asked Anne. "It's such a common last name."

Anne was staring after the limosine. "A New York financier named William Elliot. I wonder if that's father's protégé who left the bank under unfriendly conditions."

"We should ask him," Mary suggested.

Anne smiled. "If he's the man that irritated our father as much as this protégé did, I wouldn't bring it up. If I remember correctly, for at least a year afterwards he was wandering around the apartment shouting that he'd been betrayed, and he'd kill him if he ever saw him again."

"Well, you should text Elizabeth and ask her what she knows," Mary suggested.

"You can, if you like," Anne declined to take up the issue, seeing no need to get her father and sibling riled up.

"Your phone is nicer to text on," Mary persisted. "Mine takes forever to press all the numbers enough times to get the letter I want."

"My battery is low, I'll have to do it when I've had a chance to charge my phone." Anne gave up and lied, hoping Mary would forget about the issue later.

Freddie's phone started ringing, providing a welcome distraction. There was a brief exchange, then Freddie hung up. "That was Harville. They are getting the cars and picking us up. Since the house tours don't start for an hour yet, they say we really need to do the Cliff Walk."

Mary looked worried. "We're not exactly dressed for rock climbing."

"I doubt it's rock climbing, Mary, they know we're not dressed for it." Charles tried to reassure her. "And I can't imagine something like that being open in December."

"Well, you can ask them yourself more about it, here they come!" Freddie exclaimed.

Everyone bundled back into the cars they had ridden in before, although Jamie insisted that Anne ride in the front seat this time, so they could continue their discussion of poetry.

When they had parked the cars, and were following the signs to embark upon the Cliff Walk, George Harville sidled up to Anne. "Do you realize you're a miracle worker?"

"If you say so," Anne laughed uncertainly. "What miracles have I worked?"

"I have not seen Jamie Benwick look so animated...since before Frank died." He took her arm, earnestly. "Are you sure you can't stay longer? You're doing Jamie such a world of good. I'm sure we can have Jamie scoot her things over after Wentworth – I mean, Freddie – leaves. You girls can stay up all night giggling and talking about poetry and boys."

Anne did not have a chance to demur, for Jamie Benwick was hurrying to catch up with them, calling Anne's name. "Do you remember Lord Byron's *Ode to the Ocean*? 'Roll on, thou deep and dark blue ocean – roll!"

"Ten thousand ships sweep over thee in vain," Anne continued the next line.

"Actually, it's ten thousand fleets," Jamie corrected her. "All the more imposing in scale."

"I will leave you two to talk poetry, then," Captain Harville left them with a significant look at Anne.

They hadn't gotten very far in their discussion when Henry and Louis skipped up to them, giggling, and insisting that the girls be timekeepers while they raced down and back up the forty steps. "We wanted Freddie to do it, but she doesn't have a second hand on her watch," Louis told them. "So she can be the judge who tells us when to go."

Anne and Jamie held their wristwatches at the ready, Freddie held up her hand, then dropped it while yelling "Go!" to start the race. The boys ran to the bottom, touched the wall, then raced back up again. Louis won by a mere three seconds. He challenged Henry to a rematch.

"I think that's quite enough of that," Freddie disagreed. "That granite is slippery, and one of you two maniacs is going to slip and fall, and that will be the end of our pleasant excursion."

"Nonsense!" Louis grinned up at her. "You just need shoes with enough traction. See?" He demonstrated his prowess by doing rapid grapevines down several of the steps, then back up again. "Why don't you race me, Freddie?"

"No, thank you," Freddie laughed at him. "I've been through Basic, I have nothing to prove."

"Did you have to do stuff like this during Basic Training?" he asked, persisting on showing off for her by doing another set of grapevines down the steps.

"Yes, and worse, and for much longer," Freddie affirmed. "Now come back up, the rest of the group is moving on, they want to admire a great big mansion on the hill behind us."

Louis shrugged good-naturedly, and started jogging back to the top. When he was three steps from the top, however, he lost his footing. Anne and Freddie shrieked together when Louis fell over backward, and tumbled all the way down the stairs until his head landed with an audible thunk against the brick wall at the bottom.

What happened next was a blur. Freddie and Jamie raced down the stairs, shoulder to shoulder. They had been about to lift Louis' body when Anne shouted, "Don't move him!" Mary started screaming, "He's dead!" hysterically, over and over, while Charles and Henry tried to calm her.

Mr. and Mrs. Harville had been walking farther up the path from the rest of the party, since Captain Harville was slower than the rest of them. They were now out of sight, and didn't know what had happened. Anne sent Henry to fetch them, and asked Jamie to call 911 and wait by the street for the ambulance to lead the EMTs to Louis.

Then there was nothing to do but wait. Freddie looked surprisingly distressed for a soldier who had been through military first aid classes and spent time on active duty. Somehow, through it all, Anne felt this odd calmness, like the quiet on the inside of a hurricane. She tried to reassure Freddie. "You checked his pulse, right? He's not dead?"

Freddie looked at her, the blue eyes full of worry. "Yes, he's got a pulse. And you can see he's breathing." She frowned, looking down at Louis. "Figures, I really sucked at first aid. I'm a pilot, not a nurse. I actually threw up the first time I saw blood. At least I didn't faint. I had a classmate who fainted. The beefiest tough guy in class, and he couldn't look at blood."

"Well, if you need to not be here, I'll stay with Louis," Anne offered. "You go stand with Jamie to flag down the ambulance."

Freddie stood up, and took one last look at the ocean past the wall where Louis was lying. "Oh god, what are his parents going to say? If he's got a brain injury and he can't finish law school, his parents are never going to speak to me again."

"No need borrowing trouble, I'm sure we'll find plenty as it is. Try not to let your imagination make things worse than they really are," Anne tried to be soothing. "Go help Captain Benwick."

Freddie turned to comply, then threw a last look over her shoulder at Anne. "I'm tired of having parents telling me I've screwed up their children's lives." Then she resolutely climbed the forty granite steps.

Mary was still sobbing and shrieking at the top of the stairs. When Freddie made it to the top, Charles got alarmed, unceremoniously leaned his wife against the rock wall, and hurried as carefully as he could down to Anne and Louis. He knelt down next to Anne. "Is he going to be all right? What can I do?"

Anne looked up to see a crowd of people forming at the top of the stairs, staring down at them. A flash of annoyance ran through her brain. "You can make all those people go away, so that when the EMTs get here they don't have to claw their way through a gaggle of looky-loos."

Charles nodded in agreement, touched his little brother with a loving gesture that went straight to Anne's heart, and then climbed the stairs with the same sort of careful hurry he had used while descending. Anne watched him for a moment, and wondered if, after all, she could have been the one who was married to him. He was a decent person, and she really did like him.

Then Freddie Wentworth reappeared, leading the EMT crew, and she knew it was impossible.

Anne stepped away so that the medical professionals could do their job. Louis was examined; they declared that as far as they could tell, nothing was broken and the only injury was the blow to the head. But all real information would have to wait until they got him to the emergency room. They strapped him to a stretcher, and carried him back up to street level. The entire party was waiting when Anne got to the top of the stairs. Charles was sent along in the ambulance, while the rest of the group piled back into the cars for the short ride to Newport Hospital. "I should have gone in the ambulance with Charles," Mary sniffled all the way there. "I'm Charles' wife, that makes me family, too."

"It's not a bus, you know," Henry responded with noticeable asperity. "Only one person could go along. And Charles is our older brother. If blood relations mattered, they'd be asking me to go along in the ambulance, not you."

"Well, Charles might want me along to give him comfort, you know, it's not just about Louis," Mary answered him sharply. Anne distracted her by handing her a Kleenex.

Reaching the hospital, they huddled anxiously in the waiting room. The doctor soon came to let them know that Louis had regained consciousness. He had a concussion, but they were sending him for x-rays to make sure nothing was broken. He warned them that they might be admitting him to the hospital, depending on what they found. If they released him, he would need to be awakened frequently. "Either way, it's going to be a long night," he warned.

"If it makes a difference in the decision, if he is allowed to leave the hospital, we will have him stay at our house. We live five minutes from here," Mrs. Musgrove told the doctor.

"That's good to know, thank you," the doctor said before disappearing back into the bowels of the hospital behind the forbidding closed double doors.

There was general laughter and a great deal of hugging, and tears of relief. "Oh, thank god," Freddie cried, and instead of joining the family exchange of hugs, she sat down at the little table and buried her face in her arms.

Now that the worst of the crisis was over, once the hugs were all exchanged and the tears were dried, there was a general counsel of war to figure out the logistics of what must happen next. There were protestations over intruding too long upon the Harville's hospitality, which the Harvilles firmly disputed. Charles offered to call all the dry cleaners to let staff know they would be on their own for a couple more days; Mary insisted that he should go home and get back to work, and she could stay with Louis. "Your parents can watch the boys for a few more days," she said.

The parents. "Have you called them yet, Henry?" Anne asked gently, knowing full well no one had. "They need to know what's happened."

Henry looked uncomfortable. "Can't we just tell them when we get home? They're going to freak out, and since there's not much they can do, why worry them?"

"Besides the fact that they're his parents, and they'll want to know, the hospital will probably want their insurance information," Freddie added pragmatically.

"Oh, yeah, I guess there is that." Henry pulled out his flip phone.

Everyone tried not to eavesdrop on the conversation, until everyone gave up on the pretense of not eavesdropping. The Musgroves of course wanted to come at once, but the train schedule was very limited on Sunday afternoons. Jamie offered her car to Freddie. "You can drive some of the group home, and bring his parents back with you. It's an eight hour round trip, but if you leave quickly, you'll be back before it's really all that late."

"That's a capital idea, but you should take my car. It's much more comfortable for a long drive," George insisted.

"But I have to get back to base tonight," Freddie pointed out. "I've got class in the morning. Would you be comfortable with letting Louis' parents drive your car?"

In the process of discussing the logistics, three people began yawning. Anne stood up. "Would anyone like some coffee? Now that the most stressful part is over, I bet most of us could use some coffee." Her proposal was enthusiastically accepted, and Anne left with Mary to go fetch coffees for everyone.

"I don't see why I need to come along," Mary shuffled down the corridor behind Anne.

"To help me carry all the coffee," Anne answered patiently.

"They make those nifty little carriers. You could handle it by yourself," Mary contradicted her, although at least she still came.

"Well, it can't hurt to have a backup," Anne answered.

When they returned with coffee and a broad selection of sugar and sugar substitutes and creamers, Henry, Freddie and Charles were in earnest conversation. "It should be Anne," Freddie was saying. "She has a good head on her shoulders and knows how to ask the right questions. She would be the best choice to stay behind."

They all looked up as Mary announced the arrival of the coffee. Freddie caught Anne's eye as she put everything on the little table where they were sitting. "Would you be willing to stay here with Louis while I drive everyone else home? Benwick and Harville will stay here with you, of course. They will take good care of you."

"Of course," Anne answered, realizing she was blushing a little from the warm, intense way Freddie was looking into her eyes.

But Mary was indignant. "I should be the one to stay here, not Anne!" she exclaimed.

Charles looked at his wife in surprise. "We need to get home to our children, and we do have a business to run. You and I can manage without Anne until she's able to bring Louis home."

"Well, I like that!" Mary was practically shouting, and other people in the waiting room looked up to stare. Mary ignored her entire family's efforts to shush her. "I'm family, Anne's not. I should be the one to stay with Louis! Anne is nothing to Louis. She can't sign him out of the hospital or make decisions for him. How can you possibly say she's the proper person to stay here? I have every bit as good a head on my shoulders, and I can ask the questions if you tell me what to ask!"

"Mary, we need to get home to our sons, so that Mom and Dad can come see theirs," Charles tried to soothe her.

"You can take care of them, they're your sons, too," she refused to be placated. "If Anne goes home with you, she can take care of them. They listen to her better than to me, anyway."

Try as they might, no one could dissuade her from her determination to stay behind. Charles appealed to her motherhood, and how the boys must be missing her. Henry tried logic, saying it made more sense for Charles to stay with Louis, since he was an actual blood relation. Jamie thought she might be more comfortable at home, than at the Harville's house.

The rest of the party did not weigh in on the matter, and in the end, Mary triumphed. So Freddie and Jamie and George drove to the Harville's home to collect their belongings, and Freddie pulled up at the emergency room door to take Charles, Henry, and Anne back to Brooklyn.

There was a round of goodbye hugs and promises to text the latest news on Louis if there were any changes. Then they were off.

Freddie spent most of the drive trying to cheer Henry up, asking questions to divert his attention, pointing out interesting things along the road. Her voice stayed low and calm, Anne could see the officer's training in action. Only once did Freddie show any distress, when Henry started berating himself for the idea of running the race.

"Don't talk about it!" Freddie sounded ready to cry. "I know you boys were having fun, but I didn't need to go along with it! If the rest of us would have left after the race, instead of watching Louis gloat over his victory, he wouldn't have been showing off, and the whole mess wouldn't have happened! Poor sweet Louis!"

Silence reigned in the car after that. Eventually both men fell asleep, and Anne watched silently while Freddie drove.

Freddie was the one who broke the silence. "Do you mind navigating me in? My phone battery isn't compatible with this car charger, and I don't have much charge left."

"Of course." Anne talked her all the way to the Musgrove's door. Freddie leaned her head back against the headrest for a moment when she parked the car. "Should I stay out here until the Musgroves come out, or should I go in with you? Which would be better manners?"

"Since you don't have the parking sticker for this neighborhood, you'd better stay with the car, just in case," Anne advised. "I will encourage them to come out as quickly as possible."

"All right," Freddie acquiesced, then reached over to shake Henry awake while Anne did the same to Charles.

She couldn't help feeling pleased as they retrieved their overnight bags and climbed the stairs. Freddie had asked for her help, and followed her advice. It was almost like the old days.

CHAPTER 16

Back in Brooklyn, Anne helped Charles take care of the boys, and the dry cleaning shops, and did the cooking. Amanda Harville turned out to be the most helpful of correspondents, texting frequently with updates. Louis did get admitted to the hospital for overnight observation, but was released the following afternoon. The doctor did think it was a good idea for Louis to stay in Newport for a few days before coming home.

Anne tried to explain to Walter and Charlie where their mother was, and why she wasn't home with them. "She's taking care of your uncle Louis, because he got hurt. Just like she took care of you, when you hurt your collarbone, Charlie."

Charlie gave her a skeptical look. "You took care of me when I broke my custard bone," he pointed out to her. "Mommy doesn't want to take care of people."

Anne thought briefly about reassuring him that of course his mother wanted to take care of him – but children of that age see right through adult lies. "If she doesn't want to take care of people, what does she want to do?"

"She wants to be a fireman," Charlie told her firmly.

Anne nodded seriously. "I didn't know that. Thank you for telling me."

Henry texted Anne during his lunch break to get news, then called her back a few minutes later. "I told Charlotte the news, and you're not going to believe this, she's in Providence right now for a job thing of some sort! She's driving out to see Louis in an hour."

"What a crazy coincidence!" Anne agreed.

The frequent updates from Charlotte as well as Amanda Harville, rather than allaying everyone's worry, only seemed to increase the general anxiety. After a week of dinners filled with conversation about what was going on in Rhode Island, when the news came that Louis could come home, Anne convinced Henry to take the boys to the zoo while Charles drove back to

Newport to get everyone.

"That would be awesome! Are you going to come to the zoo with us?" Henry asked. Charles agreed it would be a fine outing for the lot of them.

Anne gave them both a sad, affectionate look. "You've both forgotten, I have to leave," she reminded them. "I made plans to spend the holidays with Lanie, then I fly to Ohio. I was only the temporary hired help."

It was heartwarming, how crestfallen they looked. "Are you sure you can't stay longer?" Henry asked. "You're part of the family. It's so nice having you here."

"It's going to be so dismal," Charles added mournfully. "How are we going to get by without you?"

"Same as you did before I arrived, I should think," Anne smiled at him. "Now that Jane's back from maternity leave, I don't have a job here anymore. I don't suppose you can afford another dry cleaning manager, and to continue feeding and housing me indefinitely? I think I have enjoyed your hospitality quite long enough. I love being here with everyone, but I shouldn't abuse my family privileges any longer."

There was a great deal of warm denial on the part of both Charles and Henry, but Anne resolved to stick to her travel plans. While Charles went to retrieve the rest of the clan, Lanie Russell was coming to pick Anne up.

The next morning, she helped Henry pack up the boys and get on their way. There was a great deal of unhappiness when the boys realized Anne wasn't coming with them. It was only with great difficulty that the two adult males were able to pry the arms of the two young males off of Anne's legs, where they had been firmly wrapped.

The quiet after they left for their various destinations was deafening. Anne's ears rang as she paced the house, watching for Lanie, double checking that she had all her things together. She had been packing up a little bit every day, and had even managed to donate a few pieces of clothing that were now too big for her to the thrift store.

Her thoughts kept straying back to Rhode Island, and the people currently staying up there. Over and over she remembered Freddie throwing herself into the chair in the waiting room, and burying her face in her arms when they got the news that Louis was going to be all right. It was more than relief that a newfound friend was not permanently injured. It seemed quite probable that Freddie had decided to embrace the safer and more conservative side of her preferences, and was romantically interested in Louis.

Trying to get away from the agitation in her mind, she paced the house looking for something to do. She was going to miss this place. The cheerful comings and goings of the Musgrove clan were so different from the quiet of the Elliot household, relieved mostly by the sound of her father's voice, expostulating on one unpleasant topic after another. She checked the bathroom four times and the drawers in the room where she had been staying three times before the buzzer sounded, announcing Lanie's arrival.

"Anne!" Lanie gave her a hug, and looked her over. "You're looking good. What's different? Oh, of course, you cut your hair. Well, come, let's get your suitcases, let's go have some fun!"

As she drove away, Anne took one last long look at the cheerful brownstone on the tree-lined street, then she tried to turn her full attention to Lanie's gossip.

"Can you believe your father decided to live in Dayton?" Lanie asked, pulling her car onto Flatbush Avenue. "I would have thought he'd pick Columbus or Cincinnati, at least they're a little more like real cities. But Dayton? I know there are branches of the bank there, too, but can't he go wherever he wants within the region?"

"I was surprised, too," Anne admitted. "I guess there were a lot more housing choices. I was doing some reading online, looks like there was a lot of inventing that used to go on there, and some part of town has a lot of old money. At least you can flatter yourself that he took your advice."

Lanie laughed. "I guess he really did. Dayton must have been the cheapest option. Did you see the size of that place?"

Anne wondered how much more Lanie knew than she did about her father, and Ohio. Quite a bit, it would seem. "I guess I will see for myself, soon."

"For less than the price of your three bedroom apartment in Manhattan, he's got something like 6,500 square feet!" Lanie exclaimed. "Was it 5 bedrooms and 6 baths, or 6 bedrooms and 5 bathrooms?"

Once again, Anne felt oddly reluctant to let Lanie know how little her father had told her. He wasn't much in the habit of communicating with her when they were living under the same roof, but while they had been in different states, she was quite sure he'd spent the last couple of months pretending he didn't have a middle daughter. "I can't tell you. The whole move is a bit overwhelming."

Anne stared at the Manhattan Bridge as Lanie joined the cars rolling across it. She had been looking at these bridges all her life; now she was facing her last week as a New Yorker. Why hadn't she gone to law school, like her sister?

Well, that wouldn't necessarily have helped. Her sister was out of work, too, and had also left the city. She tried to return her attention to Lanie's voice. She had stopped gushing about the new house, and was expressing her shock that Penny Clay was still staying with them.

"Well, if there are that many bathrooms and bedrooms, someone ought to be living in them," Anne observed. "Is this my sister's idea, or my father's?"

"It's Penny Clay's idea, I'm sure," Lanie answered tartly. "Your father and your sister both just think it's their idea."

As Lanie went on expostulating on the topic of her dislike for Penny Clay, Anne's mind wandered. She hadn't been out of the Musgrove house for so much as an hour, and she missed them all. Even her sister. Mary was not as mean as Elizabeth, and Mary had better tastes in companions than Elizabeth. Mary was only a small part of a large household. Charles, Henry and Louis were all sweet, and fun, and looked out for her. They were fun to talk to, and they genuinely liked her. She wondered how the Harvilles and Jamie were doing, and where they were right this minute. She wondered how Freddie's training class was going, and if she was able to focus on the class when Louis was a distraction and a worry. She wondered how Louis was doing. Everyone told her he was doing well, including Louis, who texted her himself. But she wished she were with Charles, on her way to go get him.

"So, where was everyone this morning? I would have thought at least Mary and the boys would still be home. Oh, I suppose she had to take them to daycare, now that you're not around to help take care of them and the dry cleaners, too."

Anne had to explain that Mary was out of town at the moment, and then she had to explain why Mary was out of town, and that had to turn into an explanation of the entire misadventure in Newport. Anne was very glad that Lanie was driving and had to keep her eyes on the road, so that Anne didn't have to look her in the face when Freddie Wentworth's name came up. She made much of the fact that Freddie seemed very taken with Louis, and that Mary was dreaming that Louis would soon be a military husband.

"And how is it you and Mary's brothers were all keeping company with her, in the first place?" Lanie asked rather sharply. Anne was then forced to explain the details of Freddie Wentworth's relationship to her half-sister, Senator Croft, who bought their apartment. Inexplicably, Lanie started to laugh. "Senator Sophie Croft? The one who gave that rather colorful speech when the Salander O'Reilly Art Galleries closed?"

Anne only vaguely knew about the gallery; it was something about getting sued multiple times for fraud. "I guess so. But I do believe it's possible, she's a very colorful personality." She was mystified why Lanie was still laughing.

"Well, it is a small world, isn't it?" Lanie finally explained her amusement. "My firm has been hired to go over the books for Salander O'Reilly Galleries. Larry Salander filed for bankruptcy. The court ordered the financial records be turned over to a trustee, who has to investigate the place. Lots of people claim to be owed money. I think her husband's law firm is working on an investigation. My boss has asked me to deliver some forms to them. I think they are going to accuse him of grand larceny." She looked over at Anne. "I have the forms in my car. I was going to deliver them after we get you settled at my place, but it would be more convenient to drop them off on the way. Would it be too awkward and painful for you to see the people who are living in your apartment again?"

Anne smiled. "Not at all! I would enjoy seeing the Crofts. They are really lovely people."

Lanie pulled out her cell phone. "Well, let me see if this will work out."

A mere twenty minutes later, they were walking into Adam Croft's office, only to be greeted by both Adam and Sophie!

"Anne!" they both exclaimed at once. "What a pleasant surprise!"

There was a great deal of laughter and chatter. Anne could see out of the corner of her eye that Lanie was rather astonished to see Anne's easy relationship with them. A brief stop to deliver papers turned into an extended visit. First the Crofts had to tell Anne all the details about the apartment. How much they were still loving it, the improvements they had made, the struggle to figure out where to put Christmas decorations, gossip about the neighbors and the doorman. They did admit to removing several mirrors from the walk-in closet in the master bedroom. "Neither one of us needs to look at ourselves quite that much," Adam commented. "Your father is obviously more fastidious than we are." Then the topic moved to the events at Newport, which of course they had heard from Freddie's point of view.

"Freddie says you were as cool headed as a general during the crisis," Sophie told her. "She has been worried about your state of mind, now that the crisis is over."

"I am fine." Anne tried to quell an insane rush of pleasure to know that Freddie was worried about her. "It's kind of her to worry about me. Do tell her that you saw me, and I seem to have weathered the event with no ill effects."

"I will say this for the young man, I've never seen anyone go quite so far to get my sister's attention," Sophie observed. "Cracking your head open seems a bit drastic. But it seems to be working. Freddie certainly is anxious about his health and well-being."

"Can Freddie propose, or do the men still have to do that part?" Adam Croft asked.

"Depends on the couple," Lanie answered. "Well, there is a certain romantic element to the story, isn't there? I hope it works out for them. It would definitely be quite the story to tell the children and grandchildren."

Anne swallowed hard, and had nothing to add to the conversation on that point.

CHAPTER 17

Christmas and New Year's were bittersweet for Anne: there was no way of knowing whether or not this was going to be the last time she spent those holidays in the city. She imagined she could go back if she wanted to, but there was just no telling what the future was going to be.

The sense of sadness followed her to the various parties Lanie dragged her to, still introducing her to eligible young men. She tried to hide it as best she could, and smiled through endless conversations. It didn't seem necessary for her to talk much if she didn't feel like it. People like to talk. When Lanie started giving out Anne's phone number to some of the young men from the parties, and they called her, at least she didn't have to smile at them over the phone. She just told all of them that she wasn't interested in a long distance relationship, and that effectively quelled the phone calls and texts.

One side benefit of her melancholy mood was that she didn't feel much like eating. She held firmly to her no-sugar mantra, and the plates of Christmas cookies that in the past had been a refuge for her did not even tempt her much. There were always plates of celery sticks and carrots to eat when she felt like eating. She actually managed to drop another dress size in the middle of the holidays.

On Christmas Eve they returned to the Musgrove brownstone in Brooklyn. Mr. and Mrs. Musgrove had absolutely insisted Anne must see Louis now that he was home, and everyone else wanted to see her at least once more before she departed for Ohio. They hadn't gotten the chance to say goodbye to her when she'd left before, and that was simply not acceptable.

The sounds of Christmas music, happy shrieking children, and shouting adult voices assaulted their ears almost from the curb. "Good lord, what are we walking into," Lanie murmured before ringing the doorbell.

They could hear Charles before he opened the door. "Who rings the doorbell at this house?" He smiled when he saw them standing there. "Anne! Welcome back. Hello, Lanie, so glad you could make it, too, come in, come in!" His cheeks were a little flushed; he had obviously been imbibing some holiday cheer. "Put your coats on the hooks, if there's still any room. I'll get you both some eggnog."

Louis was settled in a chair by the fireplace, which had an absolutely roaring fire in the grate. It was one of the few times of the year it got used, but Mr. Musgrove insisted that it wouldn't feel like Christmas if there wasn't a fire. It made the room a little uncomfortably warm, but after the chilly walk from the subway stop, Anne didn't mind.

Charles brought Anne and Lanie a glass of eggnog, frothy and topped with freshly grated nutmeg. Anne took a sip, and nearly choked. There was more rum and brandy than eggnog in it. Charles was watching her. "Good, huh? I pride myself on my perfect eggnog."

Anne agreed that he was a most generous bartender, then looked around to admire the room full of happy people. As much as she loved Lanie and Manhattan, she had missed the cheerful, affectionate Musgroves. Mr. Musgrove had already dragged Lanie off, making sure she knew where the food was, where the bathroom was, and wouldn't she like to join the game of Apples to Apples going on at the kitchen table?

Besides Charlie and Walter, all four of the Harville children could be seen running around the kitchen table, shrieking with laughter. Their parents sat engaged in the game with Charlotte Hayter and Henry, and were doing plenty of their own laughing. Anne was not surprised when Lanie declined the invitation to join the game. Lanie had never been much of one for small children and a lot of noise.

Mary handed her empty glass to her husband for a refill, and greeted Anne. "I see the Harvilles are here, is Captain Benwick here, too somewhere?" Anne asked her.

Mary's face instantly clouded over. "Oh, no, she's not here, and thank goodness. What an entirely dull person! And so annoying. We invited her to come tonight. After all, she's so broken-hearted, a Christmas party should cheer her up. At first she said yes, then she said no, then she said maybe. Now she's not here tonight. How is my mother-in-law supposed to plan for a party when she doesn't know how many people are coming? It's really rude."

"Oh, come now, Mary, one person more or less isn't going to make that much of a difference," Charles said over his shoulder between pouring shots into Mary's glass. "And you're not telling Anne the whole story." He shook the carton of eggnog, then poured some in Mary's glass.

"There is no rest of the story," Mary insisted.

Charles grated the nutmeg into Mary's glass and then carefully handed it over to her. "You know very well there's more to the story. Jamie Benwick has a very serious girl-crush on you, Anne. When we invited her, she said yes, but the next thing she said was, 'Is Anne going to be there?' Mary didn't know, so she said she didn't think so. I have no idea why she'd say that. Of course you'd come on Christmas Eve!"

Mary frowned. "There was absolutely no reason to assume Anne was going to come. She and Lanie could easily have had other plans. I'm not going to make presumptions!"

Anne assured them that of course she would always make them a priority. They were family. She then admitted herself flattered by Jamie's friendship.

"See?" Charles beamed at her. "I knew that's how it would be. And, oh, it's more than just friendship. She's constantly talking about you. Or maybe it's more accurate to say she's talking about the books you recommended. She finished the first one, and is looking forward to discussing it with you, and was going on about the characters and stuff. Since I didn't know what book she was talking about, the whole thing made no sense to me whatsoever. But later I overheard her talking about you with Henry. You are all elegance and sweetness and beauty. Yes, you have a very, very serious admirer."

Lanie walked up just in time to hear the last sentence, and her face lit up with interest. "Anne has an admirer? She's been holding out on me? Do tell!"

Mary rolled her eyes. "Charles thinks that Jamie Benwick is a lesbian, and in love with Anne. Have you ever heard of anything so stupid?"

"It's not stupid," Charles stood by his opinion. "She is completely agog with admiration for Anne. I don't know if it's romantic love, or platonic love. But she is passionate in her approval."

Mary frowned and shrugged. "I never heard Captain Benwick talk about Anne at all. I think it's wishful thinking on your part. I wish you could have been there, Lanie, to see for yourself."

Lanie agreed. "I do wish I could have been there. Such different eyewitness accounts as these are rather intriguing. I'm sure I would like to meet this Captain Jamie Benwick."

Charles giggled. "Oh, I'm sure you will get the chance! If she is this taken with Anne, she will have to come down for a visit at some point. Then you can draw your own conclusions."

"Any acquaintance of Anne's will always be welcome," Lanie answered. Anne detected the smallest touch of frost in her voice, but it was lost on

Mary and Charles, who were wrapped up in their disagreement.

"You will enjoy her a great deal," Charles said warmly. "She's got a sharp mind, which is no surprise; she's such a bookworm. Even more so than Anne is, and that's saying something."

"You will not like her," Mary contradicted him firmly. "Besides, she's more my acquaintance than Anne's, I've seen a lot more of her while I was up there and Anne came back here."

"Well, as your joint acquaintance, then, I shall still be happy to meet her." Lanie looked around the party. "Speaking of acquaintances, I see Captain Wentworth isn't here? From what Anne said, I thought she'd be here with Louis."

Mary shrugged indifferently. "I think she's visiting her brother in Pittsburgh for Christmas. Louis and Henry might have told me more, but I confess I wasn't paying attention." The subject did not interest her much, so she turned to Anne. "Anne, did you tell Lanie about bumping into that guy in Newport, the one with our last name? William Elliot? We were wondering if our father knew him."

"If it's the William Elliot your father did know, I hope you didn't talk to him overmuch. Not exactly a person you would want to associate with." There was so much acid dripping from Lanie's voice, even Mary did not fail to notice it, and neglected to continue with the report of how handsome he was, and he had a limousine.

CHAPTER 18

The house that Walter Elliot had purchased was in a suburb of Dayton called Kettering. Surrounding them was a sprawling neighborhood full of gently rolling hills, manicured lawns, and mansions that might look small compared to The Breakers in Newport, but certainly seemed huge to someone coming from a Manhattan apartment.

Anne was surprised at how happy her father and sister were to see her. They were eager to give her a tour of the house and grounds, which were sufficient to satisfy even their collective vanity. "We really wanted to live in Oakwood," her sister explained, although that explanation meant absolutely nothing to Anne. "That's where all the old money is. But then we found this place, and it's barely over the border. Most people don't realize we aren't in Oakwood. We're even in the Oakwood school district. Most of Kettering is very working class."

They made Anne come through the front door, so she could get the full experience of the front window that stretched an extra story above the door, and admire the staircase-wrapped foyer that was bigger than their living room in New York. The living room was separate from a great room at the back of the house, which was separate from a basement space set up with a bar, and a complete wine cellar full of wine racks, and a special wine refrigerator. There was a full dining room, and a sunny little breakfast room overlooking the pool, and a separate space off the kitchen with a table and chairs. The kitchen was enormous, and would have been a dream for people who liked to cook. It seemed a shame to waste such a beautiful kitchen on the Elliot family.

Besides the bar and wine cellar, the basement also included a large workout room with two walls of full-length mirrors, and a pool table in a room with copious empty space. "The previous owners left us the pool table so they wouldn't have to move it," Walter ran a hand over the beautifully finished woodwork. "But they took the ping pong table with them."

"Much to the chagrin of everyone from the bank," Elizabeth chimed in. "When we threw our first party, they were disappointed to hear there used to be one." She sighed. "I swear, we are buying things for the house as fast as we can, but it's going to take us years to fill all this space."

"The idea of moving out here was to economize, not spend money as fast as we can," Anne ventured, although she knew such a thought would not be very welcome.

"That's why we decided to buy here, instead of Cincinnati or Columbus," Elizabeth took Anne's observation surprisingly well. "We paid cash for this place, and we've been using the rest of the money from selling the apartment to buy furnishings. It takes a long time to shop. Penny Clay has been an absolute angel. I'm working at a law firm downtown, so I don't have any time. She has been our interior designer and household manager and social secretary. She ran out and found patio furniture before the first party, or it would have been an absolute embarrassment. She also found the house cleaners, and gardening service, and pool cleaning people."

"Speaking of patio furniture, you haven't seen outside yet," Walter opened the patio doors and led the way.

Anne understood why they were willing to stoop to buying this house in a less prestigious part of the city. The backyard was an entire collection of status symbols. The patios and decks on several different levels held a swimming pool, hot tub, fire pit, another patio with a gas grill built into the bricks, and a tennis court. "I'm surprised every star in Hollywood isn't trying to move to Dayton," Anne observed, much to her listeners' delight. "This is like living in your own resort."

"You haven't even seen upstairs yet!" Her father was positively giggling in delight. "I do like your turn of phrase, Anne. This place is like living in your own exclusive retreat." Elizabeth and Walter heard a car pulling into the drive, and they walked around in time to watch Penny Clay pull into the five-car garage.

"Why would any family need five cars?" Anne wondered with some amazement.

"Well, there's no subway out here, you know," Elizabeth explained loftily. "Either you own a car, or you have to ride buses. And since everyone owns a car, only the marginally employed or, I don't know, homeless people ride the buses."

Penny greeted Anne with her usual sweet pleasantries. "Welcome to your new home, Anne. I've been working on your bedroom this past month, I hope you like what I've done with it."

"Of course she will," Walter chimed in with a warmth that would certainly have made Lanie raise an eyebrow. "You are a wonder with paint and wallpaper and drapes and all that stuff. We were just about to show Anne the upstairs. Now that you're here, you can show off your handiwork, yourself."

It was a gallant offer, but Elizabeth and Walter did all of the talking as they showed off their bedrooms, the spacious attached bathrooms, and the giant walk in closets. One of Penny's virtues in her father and sister's eyes, Anne was sure, was that she didn't talk much.

The huge amount of space everywhere was something to be astonished by. "I've been in clothing stores smaller than these closets," Anne was able to offer honest admiration.

"Yours is smaller, but Penny thought you wouldn't mind having the Jack and Jill bath, because we have a surprise for you on the other side," Elizabeth surprised Anne by saying.

They let Anne walk into her room first. It seemed nice enough, smaller than the other two rooms, but at least three times the size of her room in New York. The closet was not a huge walk-in like the other two rooms had, but was still more than she had ever lived with. The Jack and Jill bathroom was also less grand than her father and sister's baths, but certainly more than adequate. She passed through the far side, and she stopped in surprise.

The bedroom on the other side had been turned into an office, but across from Walter's desk and computer was a wall full of bookcases. On the shelves, her books had been nicely arranged. "I have a library?" she exclaimed in delight.

"Well, there was this whole room, and I didn't need much more than the corner for a desk, and we liked the furniture, so we figured we might as well get the whole set. Nothing else to be done with the room, so we put your books here. Everything has to go somewhere." Walter was admiring his hair in the mirror that was hanging next to the door. "I hope the arrangement pleases you."

Anne refused to let the casual explanation that her "surprise" was really more of an afterthought diminish the fact that she had a library. "This will be quite lovely. I just need a reading lamp by the chair, and this will be a wonderful room to read in."

"I thought about shelving the books with the spines facing in, so there would be a nice uniform whiteness on the shelves," Penny was surveying the shelves critically. "There's such a disarray of colors to your books. But I thought I'd hold off until you got here, so that you would know where things are if you wanted to find a particular book. I can help you flip them all."

"Thank you, no, they are fine the way they are," Anne hastily assured her. Only now did she realize all the books were filed Trinity College style, by size, instead of by subject matter. Once her family wasn't watching, she would be able to rearrange them. "I wouldn't presume upon your time. You must have other projects you are working on."

"Well, now that your room is done, I had been thinking she should work on the front parlor, since it's the first thing people see when they walk in the house. But William Elliot insists it ought to be the bar, since that's where people congregate. And people notice that we simply don't have enough wine bottles in all those wine racks."

"Well, it takes a while to build up a wine collection, I should think, and people would understand," Anne stopped. "Who is William Elliot?"

"Surely you remember William!" her father exclaimed. "He was my protégé back in New York. Turns out he's been living here in Dayton for the last year!"

"And you're on speaking terms?" Anne ventured the question, feeling somewhat mystified.

"We are both adults, we can let bygones be bygones," her father waved his hand dismissively. "In the end, he had something there about subprime mortgages. It's not the first time two people in the financial industry had a disagreement about how to conduct business. But he came to see me as soon as he heard I was in town, and he has made the move here as pleasant as he possibly could."

"He has introduced us to everyone who is anyone in this town!" Elizabeth gushed. "Just last week we met Amanda Wright Lane. She's the great granddaughter of the Wright Brothers, and everyone wants to know her. She's like a local rock star. And before that we got to meet Carl Lindner from Cincinnati, he's worth a couple billion dollars."

Anne thought about pointing out to Elizabeth that neither of the Wright Brothers ever married, so the person they met was probably not a granddaughter. Instead, she nodded.

"Yes, Ohio has turned out to be something of a pleasant surprise," Walter Elliot concluded. "There is far more money in this city than I'd ever realized possible."

"And William has certainly helped a great deal to make it pleasant here," Penny giggled.

"What an amazing man! He belongs to both the Dayton Country Club AND the NCR Country Club," Elizabeth enthused. "He's got friends in both of them, so he decided he didn't want to choose whom he could play golf with. He can keep up with us when we go running. He's got an excellent physique. And he has exquisite taste in clothes."

"A tolerably good-looking fellow," their father chimed in. "Although I fear he used to be a smoker, so his skin is already getting wrinkled. He uses his face too much. He's already got crinkles around his eyes. When he gets a little older, and he loses his elasticity, age is going to go very badly for him." He examined his own face in the mirror again. He certainly did not have an excessive number of laugh lines around his eyes.

"You know, I might have seen him ever so briefly in Newport, while I was there," Anne volunteered.

"No, he couldn't have been," Elizabeth's face went so quickly from smiling to frowning, Anne feared there might be permanent damage.

"Isn't his wife's family from Newport?" Anne asked. "That's what I was told. He literally bumped into me on the street."

"Well, maybe you were told wrong," Elizabeth snapped. "What would he be doing in Rhode Island? His wife has been dead for a while now."

Anne didn't see the point in continuing to argue about it. Besides, she could easily be wrong. She was merely told by someone standing next to her what his name was. That person could easily be mistaken.

The ringing of the doorbell definitively ended the argument. She saw Elizabeth and Penny exchange significant glances, then broke into giggles again. "You don't suppose?" Penny asked.

"He said he might," Elizabeth answered, then they both scurried from the room. Anne could hear them racing down the stairs. They reminded her for all the world of a couple of teenaged girls. She was surprised to see her father hurrying eagerly in their wake.

She wandered along behind them, curious to see who could create such a stir in the household. From the top of the stairs, she watched as her sister talked to the very man who had run into her in Newport!

What a very, very small world we live in, she thought to herself as she descended the stairs.

William Elliot had stopped by to return a bag of gym clothes lent to him by Walter. "Thank you so much for the rescue. If you hadn't had spare clothes in your car, I would have had to work out in my suit. Of all days to forget my gym bag!"

"Glad to be of service, of course," Walter answered heartily. "We would have been so sorry if you couldn't work out with us!"

"I shall take a hint from you, and start keeping a spare in my car," William answered, but his eyes were watching Anne coming down the last of the stairs. "Are you going to introduce me to your guest?"

Walter turned to see who 'his guest' was. "What? Oh, you mean Anne. William, this is my younger daughter Anne. Anne, this is William Elliot. He worked for me years ago in New York. I taught him everything he knows."

They shook hands, then William failed to let go. "This is going to sound really random, but have you ever been to Newport, Rhode Island?" Behind them, Elizabeth made a choking noise of disbelief.

Anne couldn't help but smile up at him. "As a matter of fact, yes, I was there briefly for a weekend a little before Christmas. Are you…"

"The fellow that nearly ran you over on the sidewalk!" William laughed. "You were coming out of a shop, I plowed into you while I was running to my car. My driver kept missing me, and I'd finally told him to stay still, and

I would come to him. I was late, I was exasperated, and I wasn't looking where I was going. I trust you suffered no ill after effects from our collision?"

Anne assured him she had not. He asked her what had brought her to Newport. To her own surprise, under his questioning she ended up telling him all about the excursion to visit the Harvilles, seeing the Newport mansions on Bellevue Avenue, and the trip to the emergency room the next day.

"I am so sorry your trip ended in such a disaster!" William exclaimed. Anne had to conclude that he had the sweetest, most expressive eyes she had ever seen. "I hope that didn't completely spoil Newport for you. It really is a delightful place."

Anne could feel the heat from Elizabeth's eyes boring into the back of her head. It was probably the first time Anne could think of when someone was paying attention to her, instead of Elizabeth. She could not imagine her sister approving of this state of affairs.

"I would happily go to Newport again. I am told it is quite a sight to see in the summer when the place is full of sailboats and tourists."

"My wife's family lives there; I can tell you it truly is a lovely place."

Anne decided not to betray the knowledge imparted to her by the stranger on the sidewalk in Newport. "How does your wife like Dayton?"

"I'm afraid she passed away seven months ago." His face was saddened, but Anne wondered about the stranger's speculations. His eyes were not full of the grief she saw when she looked into Jamie Benwick's eyes. Well, people all handled grief in different ways.

"I'm so sorry," Anne responded, touching his arm sympathetically. Behind them, Elizabeth made a funny sound.

"I should have told Anne more about you and your circumstances, William," she said, her voice a little higher than normal. "I'm sorry, my bad. I'm sure she never would have brought up something so unpleasant had she known."

"I was the one who brought my wife up," William refused to relinquish responsibility. "It's a shame the English language doesn't have a good word that means 'deceased spouse.' If I were to say 'ex-wife,' it would sound like I was divorced, and if I said 'deceased wife,' that would sound like I was looking for pity. Which, I assure you, I'm not. It's simply too many syllables."

"I'm sure you will find the perfect thing to say," Elizabeth answered. "You always do."

"Flattering of you to say so," William said. The look he gave Anne seemed a touch conspiratorial to her. As if he and she both remarked upon Elizabeth's sycophantic attitude, and were partly amused, partly repulsed by it.

CHAPTER 19

When Anne came down to breakfast in the morning, she was the last one awake. She could hear the others talking in the dining room, and it turned out they were talking about her.

"Now that Anne's here, I suppose I really should be getting out of your way," Penny was saying.

"Why would that be? You've got your own bedroom. It's not like you have to move your things over to make way for her," Elizabeth's strident voice protested.

"Well, I don't want you to feel like I keep sponging off of you," Penny continued. Anne wondered if she was honest, or if the reluctance was an act to make her father and sister think that her continued 'sponging' was their idea. "You know what Benjamin Franklin said about guests."

"I don't know what Ben Franklin said, and why would I care?" Elizabeth snapped. "You've been an angel helping us with moving in, and we're still not done getting this place into shape. You can't leave us now. Anne isn't going to be any help around here. She can't pick paint colors and decorate rooms. Have you looked at her? She wouldn't know a fashionable paint color any more than she knows what the clothing fashions are."

Her father's voice offered his own entreaty for Penny to stay. "You have been here only to be useful. You can't run away from us now. You have hardly gotten to see anything of Ohio. As absurd as that sounds. Once you leave here, we are going to need you to take a good report with you, and tell everyone back in Manhattan that these flyover states actually have running water and working toilets and quite a few decent restaurants."

"Even if they do have appallingly short hours," Elizabeth amended her father's praise of Ohio. Anne deemed that the conversation had drifted far enough away from the subject of herself, and it was safe to enter the room. She wished them all a good morning, and poured herself a cup of coffee.

They ignored her and continued with their pressure to induce Penny Clay to stay with them.

"So, you see, we need you to stay, to salvage our reputation back home," her father concluded. "Besides, you need to give the gentlemen here something to look at. I've never seen so many grossly obese people in my life!"

All three of them glanced at Anne. She studiously avoided their eyes and stared at the contents of her coffee cup. "All right," Penny broke the momentary awkward silence. "I won't make any plans to leave quite yet. But please, please let me know when I've overstayed my welcome and I should go."

Anne couldn't tell if it was an honest request, a salve to Penny's vanity, or if Penny was actually homesick for New York but didn't want to offend her friends. Of course, it was possible to be all three.

When Penny and Elizabeth left to collect their gym clothes before heading to the country club, her father watched her critically as she got up to refill her coffee mug. "You are looking rather better, Anne. Have you lost weight?"

When Anne confirmed that she had, he nodded his approval. "You should come with us to the country club, then, and start doing some weight training. Penny Clay has been working with a personal trainer at the fitness center, and he has done wonders for her! She's never been more svelte in her life."

Anne wished Elizabeth could have heard this conversation. It made it very difficult to believe that her father was not sleeping with his eldest daughter's best friend. While Anne thought it was a little creepy, she knew Elizabeth would be violently revolted.

For the next few months, things continued along in the same vein. Elizabeth and Walter worked their jobs, Penny managed the house, Anne looked for a way to make a place for herself in the new environment. While Dayton had not been hit as hard by the economic recession as many places, thanks to the presence of the Air Force base, there were also not many jobs requiring an English major. Anne found part time work as an adjunct professor at the local community college, which at least got her out of the house a couple times a week. Sadly, a professor's salary was not enough to allow financial independence. It was enough to pay her car payments, but that was about it.

The extra time on her hands allowed her to focus more thoroughly on her weight loss efforts. She made use of the pool on Saturdays, Mondays, and Wednesdays, used the elliptical in the workout room in their basement on Sundays, Tuesdays and Thursdays, and visited her father's personal trainer at the country club every Friday. She found a surprising amount of satisfaction in being able to tolerate longer and longer periods of exercise;

twenty minutes turned into half an hour, which turned into an hour every day. The personal trainer was less obnoxious than she was expecting, and proved very helpful and encouraging in teaching her how to use the weightlifting equipment safely and effectively.

Penny worked on wine purchases and started bringing home paint colors for redecorating the front parlor. To Anne's eyes, none of the rooms Penny had remodeled required any work at all. She wondered if Penny was creating these projects to make excuses to continue staying with them longer. Or, if she was making the house over to suit herself with the thought that before much longer she would be marrying the occupant whose name was on the mortgage.

She knew that, by now, Freddie must be finished with her training course and returning to Illinois; and if she was driving, she would pass through Ohio. Interstate 70 was a major east-west artery, and would be the most logical straight line between New York City and Scott Air Force Base. She wished she had the nerve to text her. Several times she pulled out her phone and stared at Freddie's phone number, willing herself to send a text and ask when she would be passing through, and whether she needed a place to stay. But she couldn't do it. She had no way of knowing if such a message would be welcome.

William Elliot proved a bright spot whenever he appeared. He was frequently away on business, but whenever he was in town, he invited everyone in the Elliot household to a fundraiser at the Schuster Center, or the Masonic Temple, or Dayton Art Institute. Or he would simply meet them to work out at the country club's fitness center, or for dinner at El Meson or The Pine Club. Anne watched William a great deal, with both interest and curiosity. She couldn't quite figure him out. She got a vibe from him that he wanted something, but she couldn't detect what. Why did he make a point of making up with her father? Her father had been the one in the wrong about subprime mortgages. If she understood correctly, William had been the one to leave, because he thought her father's behavior was predatory. All in all, it spoke well for William. Why would he want to make peace? She thought perhaps it was more about renewing his relationship with Elizabeth. But he never seemed to show her any particular preference. When they were together, he seemed to pay equal amounts of attention to all four members of the Elliot household. For all Anne could tell, perhaps William had a romantic interest in her father. The idea did amuse her more than a little.

That spring, Lanie Russell came to pay them a visit. "It's about time I came to see how you've settled in," she exclaimed when Anne picked her up at the airport. She was as amazed as Anne at the vast size of the new house, pleased to see how much weight Anne had lost and how well she was looking, and completely irritated that Penny Clay was still living with them. "That girl does have her own family. Why doesn't she go live with them for a while?" she asked Anne bluntly when they were alone.

"I'm not sure she's on very good terms with her family," Anne told her. "I think there's a reason she's not been trying very hard to leave."

Lanie gave her a significant look. "You and I know exactly what that reason is. You would think her parents would be aware of that reason and insist that she stop trying to be a gold digger. It's a new millennium, for god's sake. Young women aren't going around marrying old men for their money like they did in the 1920s."

"Well, you'll get to observe everyone tonight. We thought you'd like to see some of the local establishments here in Dayton, so we're meeting William Elliot at the Dublin Pub."

Lanie gave her a surprised look. "William Elliot? Your father's ex-protégé? The man your father swore he would shoot, strangle, and then drown if he ever saw him again? You can't possibly mean the same William Elliot."

Anne chuckled. "I was as astonished as you when I arrived, and father and Elizabeth were all in a flutter over him. The two of them have made peace, as amazing as that sounds."

"This sounds questionable," Lanie frowned.

"I've been thinking so," Anne agreed. "I am looking forward to getting your impressions after you've met him."

Lanie was as enchanted with William Elliot as everyone else by the time they had finished dinner at the Dublin Pub. He was charming, generous, funny, well-mannered. As they compared notes back at home over a cup of tea, Lanie told Anne there was no reason for suspicion. "It was a simple disagreement. He was proven right, but he refuses to tell your father 'I told you so.' Your father was his mentor. He looked up to him. It's perfectly natural for him to want to reclaim that relationship. Especially now that he's had time to mature and see the value of good connections."

"Don't you think Elizabeth has something to do with this return? He's single again," Anne pointed out.

Lanie just looked at her, smiled, and shook her head.

"Well, I suppose he's only been a widower for less than a year, kind of soon to be dating," Anne conceded.

Lanie sighed and continued to smile at Anne.

Even though her instincts consistently pestered her not to trust him, Anne did have to admit that she enjoyed his company. Mostly because of the effect he had on her father and Elizabeth. They were always in such a pleasant mood when he was around. She also liked talking to him for her own sake. He was so well informed on so many subjects, and they could put their heads together and discuss music, politics, movies, history, and even etymology with great delight.

While they saw eye to eye on many a topic, one upon which they agreed to disagree was the idea of celebrity. Anne could not make herself care about famous rich people. But when the local buzz brought the news that Vic Dalrymple, the third richest man in the world behind Warren Buffett and Bill Gates, was going to be in Dayton, William was as agog with excitement as her father and sister.

"I knew him in college," her father reminded them at least twice daily, as sooner or later, every conversation turned to the upcoming visit. "We had a few classes together, although he graduated a semester before I did."

He agonized over countless rough drafts of emails. "Maybe I should write his secretary, instead of directly to him," he mused.

"Now, honestly, Walter, how much attention do you pay to a person who writes to your secretary, instead of to you?" William pointed out. "Just play it cool, remind him of the classes you took together, offer to buy him lunch while he's in town."

"Do you think he'd take me up on an invitation?" Walter was actually chewing his fingernails. "We used to keep in touch, but then one year I didn't get around to sending any Christmas cards, and then he stopped sending them to me. It was years ago, I didn't know that someday he would turn out to be practically the richest man in the world."

Finally, an email was drafted that satisfied William, Lanie, and Elizabeth enough for Walter to hit the send button. That fateful moment was followed by days of agonized muttering, as Walter worried that the email wouldn't be answered, or even read.

The day before the celebrity was supposed to arrive, Walter got his answer. It was all of three sentences, but it was enough.

Good to hear from you! Absolutely, let's do lunch. Send me your phone number, I'll call you when I get in.

The entire household was over the moon. Once again, William joined her, her father, sister, Penny, and Lanie for dinner, and the brief email was the only topic of conversation all night.

A week later, Anne got to meet the third richest man in the world, and see what all the fuss was about. She concluded that money was a very odd thing, and that after a certain point, it just didn't mean anything. Vic Dalrymple was good at whatever it was he did to invest money to make more money. But he was personally rather shy, not particularly well read, not interested in the arts or sciences. His reputation for being charming and witty and handsome, Anne concluded, came merely because he was rich. His secretary and probable mistress, Miss Carteret, left a similar impression. She was no doubt once a very handsome woman, but too much time in the sun getting a tan, and too many cigarettes, had left her with a very wrinkled complexion. Which, Anne noticed with amusement, her father never, ever commented upon. Not even in private, despite his lifelong habit of abusing people's looks behind their backs.

Anne was ashamed by her companions' fawning behavior during lunch with Dalrymple, and by the endless crowing after the fact. Both her father and William started MySpace pages simply to be able to brag about "my friend Vic," and "my lunch with Vic Dalrymple." Her sister already had a MySpace page, and plastered her photo of all of them at lunch across the top of her page. Anne thought the lot of them were acting like teenagers getting an autograph from a favorite pop singer. Right down to being willing to have sex with them if they were invited.

Anne's disgust deepened when there was talk of other possible social interactions with the object of adoration. At least she was able to confess her disillusionment to Lanie Russell, who kept her head a little bit. "I see no superiority of manner, accomplishment, or understanding. They aren't witty, beautiful, or even fun to talk to. They seemed woefully ignorant and out of touch with society as a whole. It felt so awkward; it was so hard to make conversation. I would never seek out their company. If my father wasn't being a crass sycophant and worshipping not the man, but the money, he would never seek him out, either."

Lanie merely smiled, and pointed out that Vic Dalrymple was a powerful man, and the acquaintance of powerful men was always worth having. William Elliot, when Anne teased him about sucking up to such dull people, admitted that yes, he was exceedingly dull, but besides being a valuable connection to have, he would always be surrounded by influential people. So being in his company would mean being among good company.

Anne shook her head. "My idea of good company is the company of clever, well-informed people who can both listen and express themselves well. That is what I would call good company."

"You didn't describe good company, you described the best company. Good company only requires money, education, and power." William raised one eyebrow at her. "And the education part is possibly negligible. An opinion is worth every bit as much as actual knowledge these days. Look at Fox News. The only thing that matters is whether you can influence others to share your opinion."

Anne shook her head. "That's horrid, and dangerous. A well-informed electorate is a prerequisite for a democracy."

"I appreciate you quoting Thomas Jefferson, but does this matter to you, Anne Elliot, in 2009?" He sat forward and looked into her eyes earnestly. "I think you're being way too fastidious, to your own detriment. Be smart. The society of the third richest man in America and anyone surrounding him is like being in the orbit of Queen Elizabeth during the Renaissance. There are advantages to being in the society of well-connected people. If your father, and sister, and you – and me, for that matter, are known to be friends of Vic Dalrymple, there are serious benefits that come from the association."

"So you're saying it's not even about being acquaintances with him, but if people know that he's an acquaintance, that matters?" Anne looked at him sideways. "That's horribly cynical, don't you think?"

"It's not cynical, it's realistic," William answered, unruffled. "I'm sure you will get job offers when people find out your father is friends with Vic Dalrymple. You will get more invitations to more social functions. You will have more men asking you out on dates."

"You're probably right," Anne sighed. "Which says something horrid about human beings. I must say, all I can feel is irritated that my father has gone to such lengths to get himself back in contact with this man. I'm sure it's a matter of complete indifference to Mr. Dalrymple whether or not he renewed his relationship with my father. You would think my father would have more pride than to grovel like he's doing around this man."

"Your father is a smart man, and part of how he has gotten to be as successful as he has been in life is by knowing what to kiss, and when." They were talking in the sunroom, by the fireplace, and looked up when her father and Penny Clay summoned them from the kitchen, wine glasses in hand, to let them know another bottle had been opened. "Speaking of which..." William muttered under his breath to her as they stood up, with a significant glance in Penny's direction.

Anne returned William's look. It heartened her to know that William did not like or trust Penny any more than Anne herself did.

CHAPTER 20

While Walter and Elizabeth were assiduously pushing their relationship with Vic Dalrymple, Anne found herself renewing an acquaintance of a very different sort.

A Christmas card had gotten forwarded to her eventually from a friend from high school, and when she had let her know about her change of address, she learned that her favorite high school teacher was not only living in the Dayton area, she was living in another part of the same suburb as Anne.

Mrs. Smith had been fresh out of college when Anne had her as a high school teacher. While she had been negotiating her way through her first year as a teacher, Anne had been a lost teenager whose mother had just passed away. Anne could not have imagined how she would have gotten through those awful, grief-stricken years without Mrs. Smith's gentle guidance. She was a kind soul, thoughtful and compassionate, and Anne had no doubt the reason her own degree was in English was because Mrs. Smith had been her English teacher.

Laura Hamilton, her high school friend, let her know that Mrs. Smith's life had taken several turns for the worse. Her husband had died of cancer five years ago. And then, two months ago, Mrs. Smith had been in a terrible car accident, and it was currently unclear whether she was ever going to walk again.

She was now out of the hospital, and living with her parents in a small house in Kettering, just off Wilmington Pike. Lanie Russell reassured her she could find other ways to entertain herself for an afternoon, and Anne rushed to visit her old teacher, friend, and mentor.

It had been twelve years since they had seen each other. In that time, Anne had grown up, fallen in love, had her heart broken, and moved from New York to Ohio. Mrs. Smith had gone from a healthy, happy, self-confident teacher at the best private school in New York to a poor infirm invalid dependent on her parents. Life had used both of them harshly.

The first few minutes were awkward, while no doubt Mrs. Smith was shocked by Anne's weight gain while Anne was shocked by Mrs. Smith's wheelchair. But it only took a few minutes for both women to find the familiar person inside the new shell, and soon they were chatting away as if those twelve years were nothing more than twelve days.

In a matter of minutes, Anne remembered why she was so drawn to this older woman. No matter what life threw at her, she met adversity with a cheerfulness and courage that Anne couldn't help but admire.

Her husband's cancer had cost them every last penny they had, and then some. They had sold their house in The Village to pay for medical bills after the insurance had run out, then they ran up credit card debts until banks would no longer issue them credit. "So I'll never get out from under all the debt I'm in," Mrs. Smith told her frankly, without a trace of self-pity. "But what else were we to do? Lots of people survive cancer. We didn't know he wasn't going to be one of them. At least we fought with every last resource we had."

It was after they lost the house that they had moved in with her parents. "At least they took us in. His parents wouldn't. I think they thought cancer was contagious. But it's just as well. After he died, it was much less awkward being with my parents, not his. And then this happened," she gestured at the wheelchair, "and I never would have managed his parents' house! There are stairs everywhere. So it all worked out for the best."

"You have patience and fortitude that just won't quit!" Anne exclaimed. "I would be a blubbering ball of goo if I'd gone through everything that you have. And here you sit, laughing."

"Oh, I can laugh now. But I've gone through plenty of depression. Anxiety attacks. Migraine headaches. Thoughts of suicide. But I couldn't take any of it seriously, though. Why should I kill myself because the system is rigged for failure? What the insurance companies really want us to do is just die. They wish that doctors would take their patients out behind the clinic and shoot them. Then they wouldn't be costing the insurance companies any money. Well, I'm a cantankerous bitch, and I'm going to spite them and live to be a very old lady."

"You possess an elasticity of mind that is fearsome to behold," Anne cried.

"What I have are some amazingly good people around me," Mrs. Smith answered. "My father put off his retirement to help support me, and my mother has found employment for me in making jewelry. I still have my hands, after all, and everything I make she is getting into artisan shops, or putting up for sale online. She is also doing the legwork for me – if you'll forgive the pun – for helping me get back to teaching. Once we establish just how much I'm going to recover. Or not. I will eventually get back to teaching either way, the question is what schools will be able to accommodate my teaching from a wheelchair?"

"You will be back to inspiring high school students in no time, I'm sure," Anne affirmed.

"And if not, I'm sure I'll find some other useful employment. Nurse Rooke gets all over the place. Besides all the patients she takes care of, she's lived in Dayton all her life, and she seems to know everybody. So she gossips about me to everyone, and about everyone to me, which is both entertaining, and almost a form of networking."

"I'm sure she's a fountain of information! She must have the most amazing stories from what she sees as a nurse," Anne mused. "Any stories nearly as noble as yours? There must be a reason so many soap operas are set in hospitals."

"Sadly, sickness does not tend to bring out the best in people. She has plenty of stories of selfishness and impatience." She shook her head slowly. "Her overriding theme is a real lack of kindness and friendship in the world."

"That's disheartening," Anne agreed.

Mrs. Smith gave Anne a plucky smile. "There's lots of greed and vanity, too. Which works to my advantage sometimes. Mrs. Rooke is also taking care of a Mrs. Wallis, who is apparently pretty, silly, vain, and has a large disposable income to spend on the latest fashions. And she loves my jewelry. I shall have to take advantage of the situation and make a small fortune off of her patronage."

Before Anne left, the two women put their calendars together and figured out when Anne could come visit again. It turned out to be surprisingly difficult, but both women had families who made a number of claims upon them. They found a window of opportunity two weeks in the future, and already looked forward to Anne's return.

The day before the scheduled visit, however, Anne's father sat down at dinner with his daughters, bursting with excitement. "You're never going to guess about the email I just got, so I'll simply have to tell you! Vic Dalrymple has invited us to a party tomorrow night! I guess it's Miss Carteret's birthday, and he'd nearly forgotten it, so now he's scrambling together a party, and we're invited!"

Elizabeth and Penny went into squealing raptures of excitement, asked questions about the particulars of the party, and then planned what they would wear. Anne watched it all quietly, making no comment. Once the other three had completely planned their clothing, they looked over at her.

"I suppose Anne has to come, too," Elizabeth realized aloud. "What are you going to wear?"

"I'm not coming," Anne told them complacently. "I already have plans."

She expected them to be relieved and happy that she would not embarrass them with her presence, and was surprised at the indignant resistance her excuse inspired. "You have to come, you're included in the invitation!" her father spluttered.

"Since Mr. Dalrymple is your friend, not mine, I'm sure he will not care whether I come or not," Anne pointed out. "And the three of you certainly don't need me there to have a good time. You'll have a better time without me."

"But it might not be a very large party, and your absence will be noted," Elizabeth pointed out. "Why the hell do you want the third richest man in the country thinking you're snubbing him?"

Anne was tempted to ask her sister why she wanted the third richest man in the world thinking she's an ass-kissing sycophant, but she resisted the urge. She was sure her family was only asked because Mr. Dalrymple could tell they would be willing to drop everything at a moment's notice, and that happened to be useful when he had a last minute party to organize, which no doubt no one would be able to attend.

"And with whom do you have these plans, which prevent you from accompanying us to Vic Dalrymple's party?" her father asked.

When Anne explained, in as few words as possible, her visit to her favorite teacher who had fallen on hard times, a fresh round of indignant diatribes spouted forth.

"You would rather visit the old, and sick, and poor, than one of the most influential people in the country?" Her father started turning red in the face. "I must say, Anne, you have the most extraordinary taste! You would rather spend an evening with a Mrs. Smith than with Vic Dalrymple? Mrs. Smith? Mrs. Smith? My god, is it possible to have such a ghastly name? There are probably thousands of Smiths in every town in America, all living on welfare."

"This particular one happens to be a lovely, gentle soul who has inspired countless children in her classroom. If my visit cheers her up while she's fallen on hard times, I should think my time is well spent," Anne answered unflinchingly. She wished Lanie was there to back her up, but Lanie had struck up something of a romance with someone they'd met at the country club, and she was out on a dinner date.

"That's fine, if you need to visit sick old people, but you can do that anytime. You can tell her something came up, and you will see her later." Her father glared at her. "It's not like she's on her deathbed, is she? How old is she, anyway?"

"I have no idea, maybe in her thirties? It doesn't matter," Anne answered. "She was my teacher, so obviously she's older than me. She's not on her deathbed, but between our schedules we had a hard time finding time that suited us both. Tomorrow night works, and I'm going to keep my date with her."

"Well, you'd better take a cab to go see her, not one of our cars," her father continued in a huff. "Imagine, parking one of our cars in that part of Kettering! They've probably never seen a Mercedes or a Bentley. The car would probably get vandalized, or stolen. All because you want to go see a poor widow in her thirties welching off her friends and family and expecting them to support her, instead of getting a job and supporting herself. Why don't you start bringing her with you to events, while you're at it? Buy her a car? Or just let her move in with us, why don't you, and she can welch off us?"

As Walter's description of Mrs. Smith began to sound more and more like a description of Mrs. Clay, Penny's face turned progressively whiter. In the midst of Walter's last speech, she felt the need to quietly get up from her chair and vacate the room. Anne watched her go, and contemplated the similarities of situation between the two widowed women, both without means of support, navigating their way in the world. Anne wondered if Penny was on welfare. She probably was.

Anne kept her appointment, as her family members kept theirs. She waited until the others left for the party, and grimly smiled as she grabbed keys off the wall and drove the BMW into the objectionable neighborhood. She and Mrs. Smith enjoyed a quiet night watching movies and sharing a small pizza, and Anne was home before the rest of her family and Lanie came back, full of news about their evening among the rich and famous.

Anne was cynical in guessing that only her family was willing to drop everything to go to a party, if it was being thrown by Vic Dalrymple. Apparently quite a few other people were also willing to reschedule their plans, in order to have a chance to attend a party for his secretary and mistress.

Walter and Elizabeth described the people in attendance, the food, the luxurious suite on the top floor of the Crowne Plaza downtown. "I am endlessly surprised at some of the nice things to be found in such a little city," Elizabeth said with satisfaction. "Most pleasantly surprised, considering what a backward little place this is."

After Walter and Elizabeth had a chance to relate everything everyone said to them, who said what, and how much money each person had been worth, they retired to bed, leaving Lanie and Anne to sit up with a pot of tea and more personal gossip.

"William and I had a very nice conversation about you, Anne," Lanie told her eagerly.

"Was he there?" Anne asked, setting out the milk and Splenda next to the teapot.

"He specifically came because your father told him that you were going to be there," she told her. "I told him all about your prior engagement, and the nature of your friendship with your old teacher. He was disappointed to miss you, but was delighted to know you are the sort of person who would turn down an invitation to a fashionable party to keep your promise to a sick and injured friend. He told me he was not surprised by your loyalty and compassion, and thinks you are an absolute model of female excellence."

Anne's eyebrows went up. "That's rather extreme praise, I should think."

"Well, I think you are very much deserving of praise!" Lanie squeezed Anne's hand where it lay on the table. "You have been far too overlooked for far too long. You are every bit as sweet and intelligent and charming as your dear mother. But while she was the toast of New York, here you are languishing away in an obscure corner of Ohio. You deserve your time to shine. William has the means to put you back in your proper place in the universe. I've seen you two talking, I know he can restore your spirits. He sees you for who you are, and would give you love and respect as well as all the opportunities presented by his money and connections. It would make me so happy to see you dating someone so worthy of you! I'm sure your mother would be as pleased and excited by the prospect as I am."

Anne sipped her tea for a moment in silence. "I do like Mr. Elliot," Anne answered after some consideration. "But we barely know each other. I can see in your mind's eye you've already got us married and heading off on our honeymoon. Please don't rush things. When we know each other better, we may not suit each other at all."

Anne knew perfectly well that Lanie knew that William Elliot would never suit Anne. But apparently they were never going to talk about Anne's preferences openly. Loving Lanie like a second mother, it was a hard thing for Anne. She longed for an honest conversation, which Lanie made clear was impossible. The best Anne could do was argue against William Elliot on his own qualities.

"Don't you find him just a little too..." Anne searched for a word. "Ingratiating? He always says the right thing. He pleases absolutely everybody. He can get along with father and Elizabeth, and you, and Penny Clay. He's agreeable, but is he honest? Have you ever seen him disagree with someone? No one agrees with everyone all the time. But he seems to. When we're in public, he can agree with Republicans and Democrats, Buckeye fans and Michigan fans. It's like he's always guarding every word he ever says. How can I trust his sincerity, if all he ever tells people is what they want to hear?"

"Only you could find fault with a man for being too agreeable!" Lanie exclaimed, laughing. "Perhaps you distrust him because he can be so unlike your father. Don't throw away a good thing, simply because it's unfamiliar."

Anne regarded her silently, wishing Lanie would have taken her own advice all those years ago.

CHAPTER 21

Anne had been neglecting her email dreadfully. She tried to stay on top of it, but unfortunately new emails came in every day. The longer she put off sitting down to read, answer, and delete emails, the more incentive there was for neglecting email, since the in basket kept getting fuller, and fuller, and fuller.

While everyone in the house was occupied with other activities, Anne steeled herself to the task of going through several hundred unread emails.

Buried among the emails was a long missive from her sister that she had overlooked a month ago. She was going to need to write a very apologetic note, and she was still going to hear about it for a long time. Perhaps it would be better to remain silent and not answer it, and if Mary commented, as she was sure to, she could claim she'd never received it at all.

> Hello Anne,
> I know you're having too much fun in Dayton to bother to write to me. I mean that with all due sarcasm, since what on earth can there possibly be to do in Ohio? And to think how horrified father was when I got married and moved out of the city to Brooklyn.
> We have all been getting by here since the holidays. It's been the mildest winter you can imagine, we've only had the littlest bit of snow. Apparently it's the least snowy winter since 1933.
> Charlotte Hayter has been coming over much too often lately. Henry really needs to tell her to go away, I'm afraid he's getting to like the idea of going out with her. It's kind of appalling.
> Speaking of people hanging out together a lot, Elizabeth tells me you are all wild for William Elliot, and he's practically one of the family these days. I wish I could meet him too, but of course I have

my usual luck. Whenever there's something interesting going on, or someone interesting to meet, I miss out. I hear you all got to meet Vic Dalrymple, and that he's bosom friends with Father. But I notice Father doesn't invite me to come out there to see the new place, or to meet rich celebrities. I'm always the afterthought with him. It's not fair. He wanted me to get married, so I did, and now I miss out on all the fun. You'd think he'd want me to bring his grandchildren for a visit once in a while. Maybe Vic Dalrymple would like to meet Father's grandsons.

Elizabeth also says that Penelope Clay is STILL staying with her. How long has it been now? I mean, seriously, it's been absolutely months. Does she never plan on leaving? I suppose as long as she's there, I'm never going to get invited to come, since where would I stay, if she's in "my" room? Is there room for me to stay, even if Penny is still visiting? I don't have to bring the children. I could leave them with Charles' parents, and come by myself.

Of course, I couldn't travel right now, I've got the worst sore throat. It's going around town. The boys got sick after playing with the Harville children, and then of course I had to get it worse than any of them.

Charles looked over my shoulder and saw that I was writing to you, and sends his love. I suppose you should also assume love from everyone upstairs, too. They haven't had us over for dinner for nearly a week. I've been getting takeout for so many days, I'm going to forget how to cook.

Love, Mary

While Anne contemplated her strategy for getting as little grief as possible for not responding in a timely fashion, she went back to her inbox. The next thing was another email from Mary, dated the next day. Expecting a lecture on her poor manners, especially her lack of sympathy for Mary's sore throat, Anne steeled herself and clicked it open.

I realized I haven't said anything to you about Louis! You are absolutely NOT going to believe this.

Louis is now dating Jamie Benwick! They are serious enough about this relationship, Jamie is actually planning on moving to New York, and they are getting an apartment together! Can you believe it? I was absolutely floored when he told me. I thought he must have taken brain damage from his accident and was imagining things. Did you ever see a hint of anything between them when we were in

Rhode Island? I confess, I never did. If anything, I thought maybe Jamie was into girls, she seemed to like you an awful lot. So who knows what you would have done if it turned out she liked you. That would have been weird and awkward.

Everyone in the Musgrove family is very pleased, and thinks that this will be a good thing for Louis. Since Jamie doesn't have a job yet, she's insisting they get their apartment in Greenwich Village so that Louis can walk to law school. None of us had any idea that Jamie Benwick was as well off as she is. But she's looking at some VERY nice places.

Charles is wondering what Captain Wentworth thinks of all this, if indeed she knows. He thinks Louis is being a jerk, after leading Freddie on for so long. You know I never thought Freddie was interested in him, so what's wrong with him falling in love with someone else? Besides, Captain Wentworth is still active military, and isn't likely to be staying in one place anytime soon. It's got to be hard to get into any sort of relationship under those circumstances. And Louis is certainly doing better than Henry in the girlfriend department, so I think Charles should just be happy for Louis. I swear, Charles himself has a crush on Freddie, and he's biased in her favor. But then, I could have sworn Freddie liked Henry, and none of us have heard anything from Freddie. After seeing so much of her, I must say I find this neglect more than a little rude.

Anne sat back in her chair to digest the news, when her father came in to use his computer. "Do I need to go away and come back later?" he surprised her by asking. "I was just coming to check my email."

Anne logged herself out and vacated the chair at the desk. "Thank you, father. I've been reading several emails from Mary, which I'm afraid I'd missed earlier."

"How is Mary?" her father took her place at the computer. Anne summarized Mary's messages, fully aware that her father wasn't really listening. "Well, that's nice," he commented when she mentioned the sore throat, and he said nothing when she suggested that his youngest daughter wanted to come pay them a visit.

She wandered downstairs, poured some iced tea, and idly watched the landscapers planting bulbs in the flowerbeds from the window of the breakfast nook.

Charles wasn't the only one who was curious about how Freddie Wentworth was feeling! What was she feeling, thinking, planning? Had she ever been interested in Louis romantically? She could have sworn no, but at other times she would have sworn yes. Has she not been texting or emailing because she wasn't interested, or was she observing a communications blackout because she was afraid she was interested? And, how did this turn of events affect her relationship with Jamie Benwick? Were they only friends? Were they still friends, or did Louis come between them? Had they perhaps been something more than friends while they were serving together? Before Jamie fell in love with Captain Harville's brother?

The questions – there were so many questions, and so many possible answers! She realized the landscapers were watching her stare at them, and she moved away from the windows. She threw herself on the couch in the sunroom, and stared at the clouds she could see floating through the skylight.

Jamie Benwick and Louis Mugrove! The cheerful, talkative Louis, and the serious, thinking, feeling, reading Jamie. It boggled the mind. If she was setting people up on blind dates, she would never in a million years have put the two of them together. Their minds were so different! She shook her head doubtfully. They said that opposites attract, but that only went so far.

All she could guess was that they started something while Louis was up in Rhode Island after the accident. After all, Jamie didn't have any other responsibilities, so she could devote a lot of free time to visiting Louis while he was in the hospital, and to keeping him entertained since his release. She speculated Jamie must have come down to visit him after Christmas, since she had stayed away from the Musgroves' Christmas Eve party.

She could imagine Jamie bringing books to entertain Louis, and if Louis didn't feel like reading, or if his head injury caused eye strain or headaches, he might have tactfully asked her to read to him. Anne laughed out loud. Of course – they fell in love over poetry! The idea of Louis, the future lawyer who had a pragmatic outlook on words, turning into a poetry enthusiast amused Anne. But she could see it happening. The fall on the stairs turned out to be a moment with a huge impact on the rest of his life, not merely on his poor skull.

She wondered how the Harvilles felt. Did it seem like a betrayal to Frank's memory? Were they glad to see Jamie getting her life back together and moving on? It had to be something of a burden having her stay with them for an extended period of time.

She remembered Captain Harville's significant look to her when he commented that Anne had done wonders for Jamie Benwick's spirits. She was going to guess that they genuinely cared for Jamie, and were glad for her.

She also remembered her sister's comment about Jamie Benwick having a "girl crush" on herself. Part of her felt sad about Louis' conquest. She liked Jamie, and if there had been an opportunity for them to explore their options together, she wondered if she would have taken it.

The other part of her couldn't help but be elated. Questions about Freddie's possible interest in Louis were put to an end now. Louis had chosen someone else, and no matter what the state of Freddie's heart, she was free!

CHAPTER 22

The Greene was a brand-new, open-air mall on the east side of the city. Anne thought it was a little ridiculous: instead of investing in downtown, the developers had created an artificial downtown, with restaurants, shopping, a bookstore, and a movie theatre at street level, and offices and apartments on the upper floors. There were streets running through it, with parking at parking meters, and even a little section that was sort of a town square. It was the place to put the Christmas tree in the winter, and have music concerts in the summer.

Anne preferred the real downtown, but William and her sister liked The Greene. The Elliot sisters and Penny met William at The Greene for a movie on a Saturday afternoon. Afterwards, they discovered the ladies' car had a flat tire. They all went for ice cream while they waited for AAA to arrive, during which time it started raining.

When Elizabeth started fussing over the long wait, William suggested he could drive them all home in his car. Anne elected to stay behind and wait for AAA, which suited Elizabeth just fine. William offered to come back and keep her company after he had dropped off the other ladies. Once he had made the offer, Penny protested that perhaps she ought to be the one to stay behind.

"Don't be ridiculous, you're busy," Elizabeth retorted sharply. "Anne doesn't have anything better to do."

Penny argued fairly strenuously that she didn't have anything that couldn't be put off for a while. What finally settled the question was the fact that the AAA membership was under the Elliot name, and Penny was not an Elliot.

The other three departed, and Anne continued her vigil with her phone, waiting for the call from AAA to say they were on their way. She bought a Coke Zero and sat in the window, watching the rain falling and glad that at least the car was under shelter in the parking garage.

As she watched a person in military fatigues approaching, she nearly knocked over her Coke. That was Freddie Wentworth walking down the street!

She wobbled in her chair in confusion. She wanted to run out to meet her. She wanted to run and hide in the bathroom. Overwhelmed by the number of different choices available to her, she did none of them. Gnawing her lower lip, she watched as Freddie met a few other people in fatigues. They paused briefly, talking and laughing, then they continued walking down the street.

Anne wanted to follow them, so she could hear them laughing and talking. She was sure she would be able to distinguish Freddie's voice from among the others. She stood up and grabbed her purse, undecided what she wanted to do, when the door opened, and Freddie's group walked in.

Freddie's eyes found hers almost immediately. The two of them stared at each other from across the ice cream parlor. Amazingly, Freddie was the first one to blush, not Anne. Anne had the advantage in having seen Freddie through the window. So all the overpowering, blinding, bewildering first effects of the surprise were over for her. This only lessened her agitation. She still stared back at Freddie with a mixture of pain and pleasure, feeling equal parts delight and misery.

There was no hiding from each other in the small confines of the ice cream shop. "So, are you going to introduce us to your friend?" one of Freddie's Air Force comrades spoke up. Freddie blinked, and introduced Anne to everyone. Anne nodded and smiled all around, and not a single person's name made it past the surface of her ears.

They all went away to order, but Freddie came back to her when she had her scoop of ice cream. Anne noted with amusement that her favorite was still chocolate, with as much chocolate chunks and fudge as could be crammed into the cup. "I thought you were stationed near Chicago or something?" she ventured to ask.

"After I finished my training class, they decided to transfer me to Wright-Patt, instead of sending me back to Scott," Freddie explained. "I was given a week to drive to Illinois, pack up my belongings, then retrace my steps back to Ohio." Anne thought Freddie's color had returned to normal, but now she seemed to be getting pinker again. "I remembered your family had moved to Dayton, and I meant to text you, but time has a funny way of running away from you. I still haven't unpacked so much as my suitcases."

Anne nodded at Freddie's embarrassed apology. "Moving is crazy, starting a new job is crazy, doing both at the same time, I'm sure you've hardly had time to get your bearings."

After they had been able to coexist among the same circle of friends in

Brooklyn, it was odd that they were so ill at ease with each other now. Something had changed. Maybe it was the absence of all the Musgroves around them, or maybe it was the awkwardness of Anne discovering that Freddie was also in Dayton. But something felt different now. Anne could only assume it was her own attitude, knowing that Louis was no longer a question hovering over Freddie.

Her phone buzzed in her hand and she excused herself to answer it. "It's AAA, I'm waiting for them to help with my car."

When she hung up with AAA, she found Freddie still watching her. "It's really raining hard now, why don't you take my umbrella?"

At first Anne demurred. "It's not far, I only have to get over to the parking garage." Then she looked out at the rain, and realized it was raining hard enough for it to be a stupid idea to pass up the offer. As she looked back up into Freddie's face to tell her she changed her mind and would borrow her umbrella, the door opened, and William dashed in, holding a large, wet golf umbrella. "Anne! Looks like I'm just in time. There's a AAA truck pulling into the garage!"

Anne gave Freddie a last look, then allowed William to drag her off. He put his arm around her, holding the umbrella over the both of them. Anne swore she could feel Freddie's eyes watching the two of them as they ran through the rain, and could also imagine what conclusions Freddie might be coming to right this moment.

William talked to her, the man from AAA talked to her, they both talked to her, and she didn't hear a word. She could hear herself responding to them when they asked her questions, but she had no idea what she said. She was in a trance, sleepwalking with her eyes wide open, looking at the world around her, but all she could see was Freddie.

Nothing confused her so much as Freddie's blushes. What was she thinking? What was she feeling? Was she really that embarrassed that Anne saw her in Dayton? Or was it the other way around? Was she embarrassed of Anne, that her friends saw them talking together? Anne had been working so hard at losing weight, but she wasn't anywhere near back to the petite person she was when they were in college. Was she embarrassed by Anne's appearance? Perhaps Freddie would have preferred to ignore her completely, but was afraid Anne would have walked up and started a conversation while her friends were watching. There were so many possible permutations and interpretations.

She wished she were a wiser person. Or more insightful. Then she wondered what would happen when Lanie returned. She was back in New York, but when tax season was over, Lanie had promised to come visit again. What if Anne saw Freddie again while Lanie was visiting? That would not go well.

CHAPTER 23

After a week, Anne's fear of seeing Freddie Wentworth again was replaced by the fear of never seeing Freddie Wentworth again. The city was so small by New York standards, but yet it felt like the odds of turning up in the same restaurant, or at the same mall, or at the theatre on the same night, were astronomically small. She was also expected to spend a fair number of her evenings with her father and Elizabeth and Penny at private parties in Oakwood, or at expensive fundraisers, where Freddie was unlikely to be.

She was very excited when George Carlin turned up on the schedule of one-night-only performances at the Schuster Center. Freddie adored George Carlin. It was out of the question that she would miss the show!

While her father and Elizabeth were not particularly fans, most of the bank where Walter worked loved him. When Colonel Wallis invited the Elliots to share a box with him and Mrs. Wallis, Walter eagerly accepted. After all, box seats meant that his fellow employees would see him. Anne happily would have gone by herself, or perhaps with Mrs. Smith; instead she found herself accompanying her family, William Elliot, and Colonel and Mrs. Wallis. They went to the Schuster Center early enough to get dinner at Citilights, the restaurant in the giant palm tree-filled atrium that served as the lobby to the theatre.

There was a problem with their reservation, and while they waited to be seated, Anne wandered among the palm trees, assuring herself that they were real, and admiring the four story-high glass wintergarden that housed them. Because she was looking up, she was not looking where she was going, and squeaked with surprise when she bumped right into Freddie Wentworth. "I'm so sorry," she gasped, flustered.

Freddie smiled down at her, then joined her in admiring the tall palm trees and the glass walls surrounding them. "Well, it is a fairly spectacular sight, I can see why you weren't looking where you were going."

"We are waiting for the restaurant to figure out our dinner reservation. Rather than listen to my father try to impress them with his 'do-you-know-who-I-am' routine, I thought I would hide among the palm trees. I couldn't bear to listen to him." She glanced in their direction. Elizabeth and her father were watching them. When Freddie turned to look, too, they both gave her a nod of acknowledgement. Anne was surprised and gratified by the courtesy.

Freddie turned back to Anne. "So do you feel like you know your way around Dayton by now?"

"Hardly. But apparently we've both found places to be entertained, between The Greene and here." Anne smiled. "It's not exactly Newport, but this place does seem to have pockets of culture here and there. We just have to find them."

"Ah, Newport. I'm surprised you brought that up. What a godawful place that was!" Freddie exclaimed.

Anne was surprised at such a melodramatic statement. "Newport was lovely, it's just that we got to watch a godawful accident while we were there. It could have happened anywhere. We can't blame the location for Louis' cavalier disregard of gravity."

"You've heard the denouement of that little adventure? That Louis and Jamie are moving in together?"

"I did," Anne admitted. "I never would have guessed that those two would get together. I hope they'll be happy. They are both affectionate and generous people. For all their differences in taste and temperament, I imagine they can make it work."

"I agree. I think they will be happy together. I envy them. They have no difficulties to contend with at home. The Musgroves are sweet, and supportive, and have welcomed Jamie into their family. No drama, no lectures about the sins of living together, they are just glad their son is happy. The only question I have is-" Freddie stopped for a moment, then suddenly seemed unable to look at Anne. She looked at the ground, and then found the palm trees suddenly engrossing. "You know Louis better than I do. Is he really good enough for her? Louis is certainly sweet, but Jamie is something special. She's exceptionally clever. She's a deep thinker, and feels things intensely. Only weeks ago, she was heartbroken. For her to suddenly be over Frank, and attaching herself to Louis, it seems out of character for her. She was completely devoted to Frank. They were perfect for each other, and you don't recover from that kind of relationship overnight. You don't, and you shouldn't."

Freddie was looking at her again. Her blue eyes were intense, and Anne wondered anew at what other depths there might be to her relationship with Jamie. She was so worried about her friend. And yet, there was something about the way she was looking at her that made the color rise in

Anne's cheeks, something about the agitation in her voice that was making her breathing shallow and rapid. She suddenly wanted to go outside where the air was cooler.

She was saved from having to think of anything to say by the interruption of her sister. "Anne! Our table is ready. Come on, we're waiting for you."

Anne gave Freddie an apologetic look, and followed her sister to their table. She sat down next to William, exchanging the typical pleasantries with the Wallises, hardly hearing a word.

Her mind floated in a haze of happiness. She had just learned more about the state of Freddie's mind than she had known for years. Now she could be fairly certain that she had never really entertained any feelings beyond friendship towards Louis. Her heart was beating so loudly in her ears, she could barely hear the waiter as he handed out the menus and took their drink orders. Freddie's eyes were so very blue. She ran the sight of them over and over in her mind, remembering the way she was looking at her while she said "they were perfect for each other." The look on her face, the tone of her voice, she might have been saying "WE were perfect for each other." Was that what Freddie was saying? Or was it wishful thinking on Anne's part? No, she was sure it wasn't her imagination.

"You're looking particularly well tonight, Anne," William brought her back to the present, laying his hand over hers where it rested on the table. "Is this a new dress?"

"Yes," Anne admitted. "Everything I have is too big, I wanted something a little more flattering."

"Well I'd say this does the job, you look fabulous," William was looking her over. "You've been losing weight, haven't you?"

Anne nodded, sorry that her sister and father were too engrossed in their conversation with Colonel Wallis to overhear them. "I've lost a lot of weight since last fall."

"That's terrific! I know how hard that is. That takes a lot of discipline." He scooted his chair closer to the table, and closer to her, while the waiter was seating another party of diners behind them.

"I…" Anne was at a loss to explain to someone else what motivated her to change her diet and habits. "was tired of looking and feeling the way I did."

"Well, you look good enough to eat," William stated gallantly. "You could be a Victoria's Secret model if you wanted."

Anne shook her head. "Flatterer."

"Is that a bad thing?" William was leaning toward her, and she was uncomfortably aware that he was admiring her cleavage.

"Maybe. What are you trying to do, inflate my ego?"

"Why not? You have the power to inflate parts of me," he said, raising an eyebrow suggestively.

Anne couldn't take his innuendo seriously. "Really, William, I hardly think this is appropriate dinnertime conversation."

"Well, maybe we can talk about it more after the show, if we go out for dessert." William picked up his wine glass, which the waiter had just delivered, and made a show of suggestively running his tongue along the edge of the glass after he'd taken a sip of wine.

There was a sound behind them of a chair abruptly being scraped along the floor, and Anne looked around. The group of diners behind them turned out to be Freddie and her friends from the ice cream shop. Freddie had stood up, and was telling her friends, "Carry on without me, I have to go."

Anne was seated close enough, she was able to snag Freddie by the sleeve as she passed. "You don't need to leave, do you? You're not missing the show?"

"Yes," Freddie replied shortly.

"But you love George Carlin!" Anne protested.

Freddie responded with a look that was as cold as her earlier look was warm, and pulled her sleeve out of Anne's grasp, and strode away.

Anne stared after Freddie's retreating back, tall and shapely and stiff. Considering where she had been sitting, she must have overheard all of her exchange with William. She ran the conversation over in her mind, trying to imagine what she might have said that would make Freddie leave.

Freddie must be jealous of William; that seemed like the only plausible conclusion. Or was it a coincidence, and she was being called away because of her job? Did military personnel carry pagers? Mere hours ago the idea of Freddie being jealous of her affections would have been nothing more than a fantasy. Now what was she to do? Should she text Freddie? If so, what could she say?

She turned back to the table and her dinner companions, and to avoid William, she buried her face in her menu. She didn't appreciate his attentions, and his flirtation certainly could not have been timed any worse.

CHAPTER 24

The following morning, Anne had a breakfast date with Mrs. Smith. She was glad of it; William had made arrangements to come over to use the swimming pool in lieu of the usual country club workout. After last night's exchange at the restaurant, Anne was eager to avoid him.

As frustrated as she was with the poor timing and proximity to the next table which had driven Freddie to leave after overhearing William's flirtations, she couldn't be angry with William. It was flattering to have him flirt with her. It made her feel pretty. It was probably the first time she had felt pretty since the day she had broken up with Freddie. If Anne had been straight, she probably would have succumbed to William's attentions. He was handsome, charming, intelligent, and easy to talk to. Nonetheless, if William was going to screw everything up between her and Freddie, she really wished he would go away.

Her thoughts wandered from Freddie, to William, and back to Freddie again the entire drive to Mrs. Smith's parents' house. Mrs. Smith's usual warm greeting always worked as a tonic for Anne. Problems always seemed smaller and easier when she was listening to you. That was no doubt why Anne had gravitated to her back in school.

"I want to hear all about the show!" she exclaimed as soon as they were settled on the back porch with coffee and fruit and croissants. "By the time I heard he was coming, it was long since sold out."

"We got very lucky," Anne admitted. "The Wallises are huge donors to the Victoria Theatre Association, so they heard about it before anyone else. My father isn't even really a fan, but he's certainly not going to turn down an invitation to sit in a box seat, at a show that everyone at the bank wanted to go see."

"Do tell me about some of his topics, I assume they were his usual blend of profanity and wisdom?" Mrs. Smith asked eagerly.

"Of course!" Anne tried to remember details. "He had a long treatise on 'bullshit' that managed to encompass population, education, and indoctrination."

"Sounds like classic George Carlin!" Mrs. Smith laughed.

Anne regaled her with as much of his routines as she could remember, frequently apologizing for her inability to do his work justice. Mrs. Smith assured her that her renditions were much appreciated.

"So, I should have realized Colonel Wallis would invite your family to join him. Did you know my nurse, Alex Rooke, also works for the Wallis family? Mrs. Wallis' mother requires a visiting nurse. Alex says Mrs. Wallis is a fairly stupid creature, but she does have a knack for knowing interesting gossip."

"I assume she imparts a lot of that gossip to Nurse Rooke?" Anne asked. "Anything interesting?"

Mrs. Smith gave her a look that Anne found hard to interpret. "As a matter of fact, she had a fair amount of gossip about you."

Anne was surprised. "Me?"

"Yes, you. So tell me, did you have any interesting conversations last night?" Mrs. Smith asked. Anne's thoughts immediately flew to Freddie, and she smiled. "I thought so. Mrs. Wallis was apparently gushing about what a lovely couple you and William are going to make. And of course there was a lot of inane enthusiasm over the fact that you wouldn't even need to change your name."

It took a while for Anne to process what Mrs. Smith was saying. "What are you talking about?"

Mrs. Smith was watching her closely. "Didn't William have an interesting question for you last night?"

Anne blinked stupidly. "William?" She desperately tried to remember a single thing he'd said to her last night. Her surprise at the question even drove the ill-fated overheard flirtatious compliments out of her brain. "Not that I can think of. Or if he asked me questions, nothing particularly interesting."

Now Mrs. Smith was regarding her with some surprise. "So he didn't ask you out last night?"

Anne was even more taken aback. "What?"

Mrs. Smith smiled at Anne's surprise. "You are every bit as dense now as you were in high school, aren't you? You never did seem to notice when a boy was interested in you."

Anne didn't know what to say, and stared silently at her old teacher.

"I'd assumed by the look on your face when you walked in here that you were happy about a lot more than just getting to see George Carlin," Mrs. Smith observed. "And since Mrs. Wallis was gossiping to my nurse about how William Elliot is very interested in you, I'd assumed that he had asked you out. It sure sounds like he was planning on it. So you're telling me he didn't?"

"No, I don't think he did. I think I would have noticed if he had," Anne answered.

Her companion laughed at Anne's answer, but then her face got more serious. "So how would you feel if he did ask you out?"

Anne blushed in confusion. Of course, Mrs. Smith didn't know. How much could she tell her? She wanted to trust her teacher, but it seemed like one of those secrets that was best told only when absolutely necessary. Anne had always felt that there was no secret she couldn't tell Lanie Russell, and look how badly that turned out. She decided the easiest route was simply to tell her as little as possible. "I'm not interested in William," she said simply.

"Are you sure?" Mrs. Smith had obviously noted her red face. "He's rich, he's charming, he's good looking. He got voted Dayton's most eligible bachelor last year, almost immediately after his wife died. There were people who had said it was rather indecent."

Anne shook her head firmly. "That doesn't matter to me. I'm not interested. Maybe he's not my type. I don't know what it is. I just don't -" she groped for the right word. "I just don't trust him."

To her surprise, Mrs. Smith sighed with relief. "I'm glad to hear it."

Now Anne was more confused than ever. "But you just sounded like you wanted me to date him."

"Actually, I don't want you to date him. But I was afraid to say anything if he'd asked you out and you were excited about it." She was regarding her with an expression that Anne couldn't fathom.

"So why wouldn't you want me to date him?" Anne asked.

Mrs. Smith's face took on a hard edge that Anne had never seen before. "Because he's a cold-blooded crooked snake that needs to be hit in the head over and over with a shovel, and certainly doesn't deserve you."

The surprises of the day just kept piling up. "So I take it this means you know Mr. Elliot?" she asked.

A bitter, angry expression settled over her features. "Yes, I know Mr. Elliot."

A chill crept up Anne's spine. "Tell me about him."

She looked at Anne for a while, as if trying to decide how much to tell her. "William Elliot and my husband were best friends in college. They met at freshman orientation, and they were thick as thieves practically from the moment they met. They took several of their Gen Ed classes together, they roomed together, they got summer jobs together. He was the best man at our wedding. When Charles and I both had our first jobs – which was when you were in my class – William spent three months living with us while he was getting his career started. Charles lent him ten thousand dollars back in those days, so he could get himself established in some business venture."

"A few years later, William was working at one of the largest banks in New York when Charles and I decided we wanted to buy a house. He was our mortgage broker. We were looking for a modest little place in Kew Gardens, but he convinced Charles that we could afford to buy a house in the East Village. Our mortgage was frightful, but he assured us that with the way real estate worked, it would be the best investment we could make, and every dollar we put in would be worth double by the time we might want to sell."

"We were getting by, but then the unthinkable happened." Mrs. Smith's eyes turned bright with unshed tears. "Charles got diagnosed with lung cancer. He'd never smoked a day in his life, but both his parents were chain smokers." Anne reached out to take her hand in silent sympathy, as she continued. "We were barely able to make ends meet with both our salaries. When Charles couldn't work anymore, and we lost half our income, expenses spiraled out of control in no time. Of course we lost the house. We didn't have much savings, since William had encouraged us to buy something we couldn't afford. We begged him to repay the money we'd lent him, and to help us refinance, to find a way to get our debts under control. Instead, he's the one who handled the foreclosure."

Anne looked at her friend with horror. "That's terrible."

Mrs. Smith's eyes were hard. "All he had to say to us was, 'sorry, nothing personal. Business is business.' I'd never seen anything so cold in my life."

Anne squeezed her hand. "How horrid."

"By that time, William had married Andrea Nelson. He was having so much fun being married to a rich heiress, he didn't have time for his best friend anymore. Never mind the handouts we'd given him over the years. We weren't asking for a handout, we were asking him to repay the ten thousand dollars he owed us. We also asked for his help restructuring our finances to keep solvent while we were trying to keep Charles alive. And of course when Charles couldn't work and he lost his job, that meant he lost his health insurance. Of course, it all ended up with Charles dead, and we didn't have any life insurance to cover funeral expenses. His parents helped as much as they could with those. But I'm still wallowing in debt. That ten thousand dollars would go a long way in paying off a lot of it."

Anne shook her head. "I've had my own misgivings about his character, but I had no idea it was anything like this. First he used you and your husband, then he used his wife. I had the impression he was doing my father favors. Is it actually the other way around, and somehow he's been using my father? Is he trying to use me in some way?"

It was Mrs. Smith's turn to squeeze Anne's hand. "I'm sorry, my dear, but it's entirely possible. I might even say probable. If you'll fetch my laptop, I can show you some of my emails to and from him, so you can see this isn't some story I'm making up for your benefit."

Anne's first inclination was to say no, she didn't need to know any more. But then cold rationality settled on her heart. "Where is it?"

CHAPTER 25

The emails William had written to Mrs. Smith showed a completely different person than the charming fellow who spent so much time with Anne and her family. He was callous, cold, even cruel. There were even old emails describing the schism between himself and her father that were downright vicious. Anne drove home with her head spinning.

She needed to talk to Lanie. What she really wanted was her own dear mother, but in her absence, Lanie would know what to do, what to think, how to piece this puzzle together. Mrs. Smith had been poorly advised, probably manipulated, and then financially ruined by William. How much danger was her family in? Her father was not a college buddy, but he had been a mentor and a father figure to William. Come to think of it, she didn't know a thing about William's own family. Were his parents still alive? Did he have siblings? Where was he born, where did he grow up? For all the time spent in his company, she knew almost nothing about him. That made her distinctly uncomfortable.

She had visited Mrs. Smith out of love, not charity for the sick and injured, but she certainly felt like the hero of a Horatio Alger tale, being rewarded for virtuous behavior. She felt grateful for Mrs. Smith's information, and sick with wishing there was something she could do to help. How could she convince William to repay the money he owed her favorite school teacher? And how could she convince her father that maybe he ought to investigate his prodigal protégé?

When she got home, Elizabeth and Penny were all in a flutter over their morning swim with William.

"You should have been here, Anne, we had our own little Olympics," Elizabeth was tossing her hair and rolling her eyes like a fifteen-year-old talking about her first boyfriend. "William is a very good swimmer. But I'm better. But Penny could beat the both of us at holding her breath underwater the longest."

"Do you think he'll ask for a rematch tonight when he comes back?" Penny giggled.

"He's coming back tonight?" Anne asked.

"I had no intention of asking him, but he gave so many hints." Elizabeth was giggling as badly as Penny. "Or, at least Penny thinks he was hinting."

"Oh, he was hinting," Penny insisted. "I wish you could have heard him, Anne. You would have agreed with me. Your sister is a very hard-hearted creature. I suppose it comes from being a lawyer. But she is toying with the poor man's affections like a cat with a mouse."

"Well, I did invite him to dinner, didn't I?" Elizabeth exclaimed. "If I was really playing hard to get the way you say I am, I wouldn't have invited him."

Anne fled to her room to avoid listening to any more giggling from the two of them. Once safely behind the door, she threw herself on her bed, and stared at the ceiling.

The questions about William kept rolling in. He had been flirting with her, and there was gossip in the air that he was going to ask her out. But at the same time, Elizabeth and Penny seemed to be under the impression that he was interested in Elizabeth. Presumably there was more to it than merely her sister's vanity.

Try as she might, she was unable to find a reason to not be home for dinner that night. She dreaded his arrival, and it required a great deal of effort to greet him with anything resembling nonchalance.

She watched him all through dinner. She had long felt that perhaps he was not completely sincere; now she saw insincerity in everything. His attentive deference to her father contrasted sharply with the words in his old emails. His manners towards Elizabeth, Penny and herself seemed like a sham when compared to his conduct towards Mrs. Smith. It took her some effort not to glare at him while he was mouthing pleasantries to everyone present. It was all so phony and artificial. She wished she had the nerve to call him out.

She realized he was trying to angle for time alone with her. He got up to follow her into the kitchen when she fetched more water for the water pitcher, and helped with clearing the table after dinner. Both times she handed him something and asked him to go one direction, while she went a different direction. She could feel his eyes on her while he was talking with the others, and he tried a few times to draw her into conversations. Fortunately, her family saw to it that she didn't have to join them.

She was relieved to learn over the course of the evening that he was leaving in the morning on a business trip that would take him out of town for the day. She wanted a day without his seemingly constant presence.

A Woman's Persuasion

Perhaps a few hours away from his charisma would loosen the spell, and she would be able to speak to her father and sister about him.

She had gotten so wrapped up in her revelations about William, she had completely forgotten that Mary and Charles were coming for a visit. Late the following afternoon they arrived, having driven the entire nine and a half hour ride in one sitting. They had brought Henry Musgrove and George Harville with them. Henry had finished his finals at Columbia and was out for the summer and wanted a road trip, and Captain Harville hitched a ride in order to go visit Freddie and see how she was getting along at her new assignment.

Everyone was talking at once while bags were retrieved from the car. The four were installed in the last two guest rooms in the basement, and then a grand tour of the house ensued. Walter and Elizabeth were of course demanding admiration for the house, and the guests were happy to oblige, except when topics about their personal lives intruded upon the conversation. Anne was able to glean through the rambling discussions that Mrs. Harville and the children were all doing well, Jamie Benwick and Louis Musgrove were quite delighted with their new apartment, and Mary was finally giving in to Charles' insistence that they put the boys in daycare. The biggest gossip was that Henry was now officially dating Charlotte Hayter.

Charles and Henry were delighted, and Mary was somewhere between disgusted and appalled. "Well, Mother and Father are delighted," Charles defended his brother to Anne when Henry and Mary were in the next room with the rest of the party. "Mother has been friends with Mrs. Hayter forever. She's like another aunt to me. If they got married, then she really would be a member of the family, and that would be awesome. And besides, I've always liked Charlotte. She's sweet, she's cute, she's smart, what's not to like?"

"Well, I'm happy for him, and happy that everyone else is happy. It saddens me that my sister is clinging to outdated racist ideas. I suppose my father and Elizabeth aren't much better in their attitudes." Anne firmly pushed away memories of the day she introduced them to Freddie. "You and your brothers are lucky to have such excellent parents. They truly care only about your happiness. They must still be worrying constantly about Louis. Do you think he's fully recovered now?"

Charles frowned. "Well, yes, I think he's fine, but he's also…different."

"Different?"

"He's quieter than he used to be." He scratched his head, looking for something more specific. "Less boisterous. He was always climbing on things, walking on the handrails instead of taking the stairs, laughing at us when we said maybe he shouldn't act quite so much like a mountain goat. Now he's less likely to be ten paces ahead of the rest of the group, looking to see what mischief he can get into."

"Well, I should think this episode may have taught him a lesson and demonstrated that all of you were concerned for a good reason," Anne pointed out.

"Well, and he's also pretty wrapped up in this new girlfriend," Charles added. "Instead of running ahead trying to show off for her, he's holding her hand and walking with her, while they whisper to each other. Or he's sitting back with his eyes closed, instead of fidgeting like he used to, while she reads poetry to him. I wonder about her a little. I know he's going to be a lawyer and all, but she seems awfully bookish, even for him. No, maybe it's not that she's so bookish, but so artsy. She never reads anything that doesn't rhyme. And she's completely not interested in sports," Charles concluded mournfully.

Anne laughed at his woebegone expression over his last observation. "That can't meet with your approval. But I do think she's an excellent woman, and they should be good together."

"I'm sure they will be. They both seem awfully happy, and very much in love. I'm not foolish enough to think that everyone out there has the same tastes as I do. Jamie Benwick is a great gal. I have to admire someone who has served in the military, AND is all artsy-fartsy and can quote Tennyson or Dickens."

Anne smiled. "I thought you said she never reads anything that doesn't rhyme."

Charles looked surprised. "I did. She doesn't."

Anne shook her head fondly at her brother-in-law. "Charles Dickens wrote prose, not poetry."

He waved both hands in the air in resignation. "Well, you know what I mean."

They were interrupted by the absolute necessity for Charles to catch up with the others and admire the mirrors and the china cabinet. Anne stopped to sigh before she joined them. They all seemed to be pairing off: Charles and Mary, Louis and Jamie, Henry and Charlotte. She could even add Elizabeth and William if she had what she wanted, and Penny Clay and her father if Penny got what she wanted. Part of her wished she wanted what everyone else did. Life would be so much simpler.

As unenthusiastic as her father and Elizabeth had been about Mary's visit, it seemed to be off to a promising start. The former were always eager to show off the new house with its endless rooms and amenities, and Mary was in the rare mood to be pleased and amazed by everything they showed her. "I wish we could move out here, too," she gushed when they stepped outside to see the pool, hot tub and tennis court. "This is like living at a vacation resort!"

While they milled about admiring the landscaping and the multiple porches along the back of the house, Elizabeth pulled out her smartphone to show the guests photos of William. Mary and Charles both agreed that he was an exceedingly good-looking man, and looked forward to meeting him.

Elizabeth and Walter had an awards dinner for work which they had to attend. "It can't be helped," Walter apologized with a fair attempt at real regret. "But I promise, we'll make it up to you tomorrow! Vic Dalrymple's in town again; I invited him to come over for a game night. I just bought *Say Anything*, and since he loves *Wits and Wagers*, it was easy to entice him to come over and try it!"

"William said he'd come too. So you'll get a chance to meet him in person," Elizabeth added.

There was a general exclamation of enthusiasm, then the topic of dinner resurfaced. Penny excused herself on account of her own plans, so Anne was put in charge of marshalling the guests. George Harville called Freddie, and made arrangements for them to meet in the Oregon District. "She says there are lots of good places there. She didn't make reservations, so we can walk up and down the street and check out all the options."

"It's a Tuesday night, there shouldn't be much of a wait, so you might as well get to experience the whole scene," Anne agreed.

The five of them all fit easily into the Bentley, which Walter left for their use since it had four doors and the roomier back seat. Anne tried to be a good hostess and point out anything of interest on the way. It was only a twelve minute drive, and they drove more past the University of Dayton and Woodland Cemetery than through them, but she did what she could. It was certainly not like showing people Central Park and the Empire State Building.

She parked at the lot on the west end of the Oregon District. "There's a good Thai restaurant on this end, a good Irish restaurant on the other end, and lots of good places in between," she told them as they got out of the car. "Now, where are you supposed to meet Freddie?" she asked George.

"Here will be just fine," Freddie's voice answered from behind them.

Anne jumped, and blushed, and was glad that all attention was focused upon the hearty reunion of the two officers. She had spent the entire drive wholeheartedly not thinking about this moment. She stood at the back of the little group, half eager and half afraid. What was Freddie's state of mind? Which would take precedence, their conversation under the palm trees, or the jealousy that drove her away from the restaurant?

Freddie's greeting to her was casual enough to make her fear the latter. She tried to remain calm. After all, they were not junior high school children, hormonally driven and chronically unsure of themselves. Yet only a few moments later, she was filled with apprehension that this arrangement, being in each other's company under these circumstances, could produce all sorts of mischief.

They all walked down Fifth Street, examining the menus as they passed each restaurant. Mary was getting impatient with the process, and only gave the next restaurant a cursory glance, before she moved away to let Captain Harville read the menu while she looked around. "All the buildings are so short," she observed, looking back towards the downtown skyline. "Oh!" she exclaimed. "There's Penny! Penny!" she shouted and waved, then stopped. "She's talking to someone. Isn't that Elizabeth's friend? William Elliot?"

"It shouldn't be him, he's supposed to be out of town today," Anne answered. Freddie looked over at her, and she immediately wished she hadn't said anything.

Unfortunately, Mary insisted on pursuing the subject. "Well, I have eyes, she showed me his picture two hours ago! Isn't that the same guy?"

Anne felt compelled to stand next to Mary on the sidewalk and dutifully look where she was pointing. To her surprise, she had to confirm that it was, indeed, William Elliot who stood down the street, talking with Penny. They seemed very absorbed in whatever it was they were discussing. "You are absolutely right, Mary. Good eye!" she tried to shrug indifferently, and turned away. "Maybe his trip got cancelled. I'm sure we'll hear all about it soon."

Hopefully that would put things in the proper perspective. Anne hoped she had repaired any damage from seeming to know too much about William Elliot's affairs. And speaking of affairs – as she turned back to summon Mary when the group elected to continue down the street, William and Penny kissed before they walked off in different directions. "So Penny's plans involved William, and she did not see fit to tell Elizabeth and Father," Anne mused to herself. "Interesting."

There might be a perfectly innocent explanation to all this, like they were planning a surprise birthday party for her father. But that parting kiss didn't look terribly innocent. Certainly if Elizabeth had seen it, she would not have interpreted it as such. It looked like William lied about his business trip, and Penny was deliberately vague about her evening plans.

She tried to focus her attention back on the party as they continued to wander their way down Fifth Street. There was a poster for Wiley's Comedy Club, and Charles was trying to entice them into going.

"We can't go tomorrow!" Mary was exclaiming to Charles' proposal. "My father invited Vic Dalrymple over to play board games! I can't believe you've already forgotten."

"Big deal! We can sit around at home playing board games anytime," Charles answered. "Here we are with a few days without the kids, so we can go out and have fun, and you don't want to go out?"

"But Vic Dalrymple is coming!" Mary exclaimed. "We're about to meet one of the richest men in America, and you want to go to a third rate comedy club in a small town in Ohio?"

"Why do you care about meeting a rich man?" Charles asked. "You're already married. Are you planning on dumping me for him? You know he's not the marrying kind, right? He just has affairs. It's a lot cheaper than wives."

"He's famous, why aren't you ever interested in famous people unless they play sports?" Mary complained. "If that's not enough for you, we're also supposed to get to meet William Elliot."

"Why is it so important that we meet him tomorrow?" Charles asked. "It sounds like he's around a lot, it's not like it's going to be hard to meet a friend who comes around all the time. Meeting William Elliot does not sound like a big deal to me. I'd rather have some fun on my vacation."

While the couple continued bickering, Anne and Freddie caught each other's eye. She didn't know how to interpret her expression.

Henry was the one who brought the argument to a close, pointing out that they were going to be visiting for several days, and there would be plenty of nights when they could go out to the comedy club.

Freddie had dropped back to walk next to Anne behind the rest of the group. "Well thank goodness that's settled. I'm sure you were breathless with anticipation at the idea of introducing your sister and brother-in-law to Mr. Dalrymple," she murmured.

Anne gave her a somewhat sour look. "I'm with Charles. I'd rather go to the comedy club."

"And miss the chance to mingle with the rich and famous?"

"Board games bore me. And the idea of playing board games with boring people does not sound like an ideal evening to me," Anne answered somewhat petulantly.

Freddie chuckled. "The Anne Elliot I knew never did spend much time worrying about the lives of the rich and famous. And she certainly never liked games all that much. Cards, board games, role playing games, none of it was ever your thing."

"I haven't changed," Anne answered, and then stopped from saying any more, unaccountably afraid of how her words might be interpreted.

"It's been almost nine years. People can change," Freddie observed. "Tell me, have you ever learned to like *Dungeons & Dragons*, at least?"

Anne never got to answer, for at that moment George Harville and Henry announced that a decision had been made, and they had settled upon Thai 9 as their choice for dinner. Now that the choice had been made, the group walked back to the restaurant – which was the one immediately next to the parking lot where their cars were.

While they were putting away their receipts after dinner and getting up from the table, Mary checked her cell phone. "Elizabeth says that father says that we ought to invite Captain Wentworth to come to the game night tomorrow. He's sorry he didn't think of it before. But since Captain Harville is here to visit her, it would be rude not to include the both of them in our little party."

Charles read the text over his wife's shoulder. "That's awesome! Will you be able to make it? You really should come."

Freddie's face was smooth and blank. Anne could imagine why. The last time Freddie saw her father and Elizabeth, they were yelling and screaming. It was that night's interview which caused Anne to break up with Freddie. "I will have to check my calendar."

"Well, whatever it was, you can reschedule after I leave," George Harville chimed in.

Freddie was still noncommittal. "I will let you know."

The entreaties for Freddie to come to the party followed her out to the parking lot. "You know you want to come," Mary interpreted Freddie's expression. "When else are you going to get the chance to meet one of the richest men in America? Whatever else is on your schedule can wait."

"I'll be there if I can," Freddie answered her. Anne was fairly convinced by her expression that she was lying to her sister, just to get her to shut up. After they all bid her good night, they piled back in the car for the short drive back to the Elliot house.

Penny Clay was already there, and Walter and Elizabeth returned shortly thereafter. Alone with Penny in the kitchen for a moment, Anne obeyed a rash impulse, and confronted Penny. "Mary and I saw you and William in the Oregon District tonight. We called to you to get you to join us, but you were both so busy talking, you didn't hear us."

Anne could swear she saw guilt flitter across Penny's face. "You saw us? Why didn't one of you run over to get us? That would have been fun." Apparently thinking that was not a sufficient answer to explain them being seen together, she continued after a moment's silence. "I was so surprised to bump into him after my date. I thought he'd said he was going out of town. But I guess the meeting got called off. I think he knew Elizabeth had other plans, or I bet he would have called to see if he could join us."

"No doubt," Anne murmured.

"He was going on and on about how excited he is for game night tomorrow. I guess he's as big a fan of *Wits and Wagers* as Mr. Dalrymple, and is very much looking forward to the new game."

"I'm sure Elizabeth will be very pleased to hear from you how excited he is about tomorrow," Anne said. Then she watched the red on Penny's face creep across her cheeks, up to her hairline and down her neck.

"I'm sure you're right," was all she said.

CHAPTER 26

When Anne came home from teaching her college class, the gray rainy day was putting her out of sorts. She was glad her father and sister were still out, and she would be able to park in the garage.

She was surprised to find Freddie's car in the driveway, thoughtfully parked far to one side, so the household cars could get into the garage. When Anne came in, she and George Harville were sitting at the big kitchen table, poring over the laptop. There was a little box open on the table, in front of them, and a beautiful gold pocket watch was lying next to the box.

"Hello! You both look like you're up to some fun mischief," Anne greeted them, kicking off her wet shoes next to the door.

"Hello yourself! How was your class?" George got up from the table to come over and offer his assistance.

Anne was surprised by the gentlemanly gesture, but turned her back to him so he could help her shrug out of her jacket. "It went well. We've been reading the Romantic poets, and of course I include Edgar Allan Poe. This class has taken a particular shine to him, which I find terribly endearing."

George smiled. "It sounds like Benwick would absolutely love to take your class. Isn't she always quoting Poe?" he threw his question back over his shoulder at Freddie.

Freddie was absorbed in the laptop. "Hm? I think so." She was intently scribbling things down on scratch paper while looking at the screen.

"Neither of you has confessed to me yet what project you are finding so absorbing," Anne reminded George, since she knew Freddie well enough to know that she was so focused on her task she would not hear her, and it was useless to ask any question while she was thusly occupied.

"I got a package from Benwick – I mean Jamie – today," George explained. He walked back to the table, and brought back the antique gold pocket watch, which he handed to Anne.

Anne took it over to the breakfast nook by the window to examine it better, then turned on the light when the gray weather refused to give ample illumination. She sat down at the little table, and turned it over in her hand. The front and back covers were etched with finely-done swirls. When she opened the case, the face not only had a ring of elegant roman numerals, there was a smaller circle set in the bottom with a hand that marked the seconds. "It's beautiful!" she exclaimed.

"Jamie had bought it for Frank. It was going to be her wedding present." George sat down next to Anne with a despondent sigh. "Now Jamie sent it to me, asking if, while we're here, we could find a watch chain for it at one of the antique malls. She wants to give it to Louis."

His face was a study in grief for his lost brother. Anne put her hand on top of his in silent sympathy.

"I don't know what I was expecting. I didn't expect Jamie to mourn for Frank forever. I should be glad for her that she's moving on. She's young and beautiful and loving, and she should be getting on with her life. But giving him something that was supposed to be a gift for my brother…it's not rational, but it hurts. I'm trying not to be angry."

Anne rubbed his hand with her own, where it lay on the top of the table. "Grief isn't rational."

"Poor Frank." George folded his lips tightly together, and Anne looked away, so that he could cry without her watching him, if he needed to. "He wouldn't have forgotten her this quickly. He adored her. Worshipped the ground she walked on. That watch would have lived in the top dresser drawer the rest of his life, rather than be given to someone else."

Anne took George's hand in both of hers now, and looked earnestly up into his face. "I believe that. But everyone grieves in a different way. Some people put less emphasis on things than others. It doesn't mean she didn't love him. We could all see how much she's suffered since Frank's death."

"Frank had the sweetest, most feminine soul of anyone I've ever known. He was gentle, and kind, and loyal. Maybe that's why this hurts, it feels disloyal. Loyalty like his would have extended beyond the grave. Jamie's masculine soul isn't capable of the same kind of loyalty."

Anne shook her head. "We've already established that you didn't expect Jamie to mourn forever. I wouldn't say that loyalty is only a feminine trait. Look at you, you seem perfectly masculine to me, and you are clearly loyal to your brother. Why do you think souls have genders?"

George looked down at their intertwined hands. "You've seen it, I'm sure you have. Souls like yours are very feminine. You're sensitive, caring, tactful, and healing. Other souls are not. They are more strong, combative, competitive, and driven. I'm not saying either is bad, but there are definitely different kinds of souls."

"You've described traits, but there's nothing to say those traits have to belong solely to one gender," Anne disagreed.

"Well, I'm not saying that being a man means you have a masculine soul, or being a woman makes you have a feminine soul. Take Wentworth over there, she's the perfect example of a masculine soul. And my brother, like I said, had a very feminine soul."

"But we all of us are collections of traits, and they can easily cross your masculine-feminine lines. It's possible to be strong, but sensitive, combative, yet diplomatic, driven, but also healing," Anne pointed out.

"Well, maybe," George admitted uncertainly.

"And if I were to concede that there is such a thing as masculine and feminine souls, I am not going to agree with you that loyalty is a trait of only one of the two. I would argue that a masculine soul would be every bit as capable of loyalty as a feminine soul," she stated stoutly.

"Well, literature would be on your side," he conceded.

Anne smiled. "But then, all that literature was written by men."

George used his free hand to lift a finger in the air. "But! The souls of writers are bound to be more sensitive, more observant, and therefore more feminine."

Anne shook her head. "We will have to agree to disagree on that point. It is possible to be aggressive, and observant. Or competitive, and sensitive. Loving wordcraft is something that I think both genders can agree on with our minds and bodies, so why not also with our souls?"

George frowned. "Yes, I will agree to disagree with you. The feminine soul loves words, while the masculine soul loves to climb trees."

Anne laughed. "And you don't know any children who used to climb a tree to go read a book?"

George stared. "You got me there. I did know kids who did that. I had a couple of friends who loved to do that."

Anne pushed her advantage. "And what about that word we keep using – love? Love isn't masculine or feminine. Love transcends gender. People may express it in different ways, but even that isn't masculine and feminine."

"Sure it is!" George exclaimed. "There are bookstore shelves full of relationship counseling books all about how men and women do love differently. Women want a guy who will 'do the little things,' men want women who will leave them alone to watch sports sometimes."

"Is that really about love, or is that more a characteristic of hormonal traits?" Anne asked. "Is that really the soul talking, or is that testosterone and estrogen?"

George opened his mouth to say something, but no words came out. His eyes crinkled at the corners while he was thinking over her idea.

"Love is the meeting of two minds, and two souls," Anne continued.

"And the meeting of two bodies. Your examples of taking out the garbage or watching sports, or whatever, that's just likes and dislikes and behaviors and the training we received from our parents. And the expectations we learned from watching our parents' marriages. Relationships are negotiated around the preferences of two individuals, regardless of gender. A man and a woman, two men, two women, what does it matter if they love each other?"

There was a clattering, spluttering sound behind them, and they both looked around. Freddie slid off her stool, and knelt down to pick up all the papers that she had knocked off the counter. "Sorry," she looked up at them sheepishly. "I'm almost done here, I've found a bunch of antique places, and an unbelievable number of thrift stores that sound like places we'll want to check out."

Anne and George turned back to their conversation. Anne released George's hand, and picked up the watch to look at again. It really was a beautiful thing. "Now, here's a question for you, do you think a relationship always has to be one male and one female soul?"

George looked at her skeptically. "If you put two male souls, together, they'd always be fighting for dominance. If you put two female souls together, nothing will ever get decided."

"I don't believe you mean that, not for one moment," Anne told him. "So I won't tell your wife you said it."

George looked at her, concerned. "I appreciate that. I would say that I have the feminine soul, and she has the masculine one, but as part of that masculinity, she would beat me for that statement."

"And I would say that just proves my point that traits are neither masculine nor feminine," Anne insisted with a smile. "We shall obviously never agree upon this question."

"Well, there certainly isn't any way we would ever be able to prove it, one way or the other, when the concept of the soul itself is unprovable," George responded.

"It is a difference of opinion which does not admit proof," Anne agreed. "And, to an extent, it doesn't matter. I value the warm and faithful feelings of my fellow creatures, and I believe all people are capable of everything great and good, no matter whether their motivation comes from a male soul, or testosterone, or a female soul, or estrogen."

"You are a good soul!" he cried, giving her an affectionate hug as they both stood up and turned to check on Freddie. "And an even better debater. There's no quarreling with you. So, Wentworth, are you done yet? We ought to get moving if the list of places we're supposed to go is this long."

"Just finishing," Freddie answered. "You're right, we should get moving. We've only got so much time, and this is a long list." She jumped up from her chair and showed the list to Anne. "Any suggestion where we start?"

"Antiques Village would be a good start. It's big, and it's close," Anne said, scanning the list.

Freddie smiled at her, the blue eyes warm and filled with an expression almost of entreaty which Anne didn't know how to interpret. "Let's be off, Harville. Anne, would you mind closing all the webpages I've got open on this, and logging me out of everything?"

Anne thought it was a somewhat odd request, but was pleased to be asked. "Of course. You both run. See you tonight."

The two captains were out the door as quickly as George Harville's limp would allow. He could move very quickly when he needed to.

Anne sat down in front of the laptop. Next to it was the stack of scratch paper Freddie had been scribbling on – and there was a long letter in Freddie's handwriting on top of the stack. Her own name was scrawled across the top of the page.

Anne –

I can no longer listen in silence. You pierce my soul. I am half agony, half hope. Tell me I'm not too late, that your precious feelings are gone forever. I offer myself to you again with a heart that is even more your own than when you almost broke it nearly nine years ago.

Did you mean it when you said that love is the meeting of two minds, two souls, and two bodies? I believe you did. And when you said that gender doesn't matter, as long as two people love each other? If you truly value the warm and faithful feelings of your fellow creatures, I can only hope that if I offer you mine again, this time you will accept them.

I have never loved anyone but you. I've been weak, I've been resentful, but I have never been inconstant. You alone have brought me to Dayton. For you alone I think and plan. Have you never wondered how I ended up here, instead of back in Illinois? I was due for a transfer. Knowing you were following your father to Ohio, I was able to put in a request so that I could follow you here. Can I make my wishes any plainer?

Please, let's begin again. I cannot live without you. I've tried, and the misery of it is more than I can bear. Will you come back to me?

Yours always and forever,
Freddie

Such a letter! Anne read it, and read it again, the blood pounding so loudly in her ears she had to read it aloud. She wanted to laugh. She wanted to cry. She wanted to dance for joy. As it was, she was able to do none of the above, for as she sat there trying to absorb the joyful news that Freddie still loved her and wanted her back, Charles, Mary, and Henry walked in the door from the garage while the cleaning service rang the front doorbell, and the house exploded with unwanted people.

Everyone was talking to her at once. The cleaning service had questions for her about the instructions for the evening's party. Charles, Henry, and Mary were all talking at once, telling her about their visit to the Air Force Museum. Charles liked the museum, Henry wanted to show Anne the presents he bought in the gift shop, and Mary was complaining how large the museum was, and how much walking she'd had to do. "I thought with all the cars out here, I wouldn't have to walk so much," she moaned, sitting at the table and kicking off her shoes.

Anne put Mary in charge of telling the cleaning staff where she thought they should set things for the party so they would be ready when the caterers arrived, nodded at Charles' comments, admired Henry's gifts. The laptop was still in front of her, still filled with Freddie's research. Antiques Village. She had told them to go to Antiques Village. "I need to run out on a quick errand," she told the lot of them, quickly closing the browsers and shutting down the computer. "Will all of you be all right here, you don't need me for anything?"

Mary made a noise. "What if the caterers get here before you get back?"

"You're in complete charge," Anne reassured her. "Whatever arrangements you make, that's what everyone is going to have to obey. I'm sure it will be perfect, you've got a knack for organizing people." She gave her a hasty hug, waved at the men while she grabbed her purse and car keys, and ran out the door.

"Wait, why don't I come with you? You can drop me at Dick's Sporting Goods," she heard Charles saying, just as the door closed behind her. She kept on running, hoping against hope that he would not follow her. She needed to see Freddie, needed to see her now, and needed a few minutes alone. She ripped the car door open, threw herself into the seat, started the engine and pulled away before she took the time to fasten her seatbelt.

CHAPTER 27

Charles did not come running out the door after her; she had made a successful escape. Fortunately it was a short drive to the antique mall, since Anne hyperventilated the entire drive. It was not from the exertion; in the nine months since she had first laid eyes on Freddie in the Musgrove's dining room, and she'd heard that Freddie barely even recognized her, she had lost almost 70 pounds. Daily exercise and the complete lack of sugar kept her strictly on her 2 pounds a week schedule. Sixty-seven fewer pounds made running a lot easier.

She was relieved to spot Freddie's car in the parking lot in front of the antique mall. This was not going to make her task any easier; it was a large place. And there were several vendors who had cases of jewelry to sort through. Trying not to run, she hurried across the front lane, looking down each aisle.

Blissfully, it wasn't too long before she found George Harville examining a large selection of teapots and teacups. "I ought to bring Amanda a present, what do you think of these?" he pointed out a couple of different teapots.

Anne could barely look at the choices being presented to her. She was frantic in her need to find Freddie. "Your wife already has several teapots, what about the cute little sugar and creamer set over there?" she asked, pointing to a sweet little matched set.

"That's just the thing!" George exclaimed. "See, I needed a woman's touch to help me figure things out."

"And you say you're the one with the feminine soul," Anne couldn't resist carrying on their debate with a shade of a smirk. "Where's your partner in crime?" she asked, trying to sound casual.

"Over by the jewelry case, down that aisle and around the corner," he pointed. "I just couldn't do it. She told me to find a present for Amanda, and leave this job to her. I wasn't sorry to take her up on that."

"It's understandable," Anne responded. When George turned back to pick up the sugar and creamer set, she hastily slipped away.

She found Freddie standing in front of a case filled with shining antique jewelry. She had the watch in one hand, and was intently peering into the case, then held up the watch to see if the gold tones matched. Anne well knew how intensely Freddie could concentrate on a task at hand, and was able to walk softly up beside her.

"The one on the left, I think," she said softly.

Freddie jumped a little, then laughed to see Anne beside her. "I was just wishing you were here to help me decide," she admitted. "The one on the left, you think?"

Anne's eyes looked up into the blue ones she would love as long as she lived. "Yes."

They stared into each other's eyes for a long moment, watch and chain forgotten. "I take it you got my note?" Freddie finally whispered.

Anne nodded. "Yes. And…. Yes."

In exquisite slow motion, the distance between them closed, and there among the shining and precious heirlooms, their lips met.

After they acquired the watch chain, they spent the better part of the next hour wandering among the dusty, shiny, priceless and unique items, occasionally crossing paths with George Harville, comparing notes, pouring out their thoughts and feelings and retracing the past, both recent and distant.

She confessed that she had wondered about whether Freddie was romantically interested in Louis Musgrove. Freddie confessed that she was sure that Anne had been romantically involved with William Elliot. They had both been tormented by doubts, by wondering if the other had honestly switched which team they were batting for, or if they were giving in to the pressures of family and society, or if their earlier romance was being dismissed as a youthful, experimental fling.

Freddie told her that her doubts and questions about Anne's view of their past had melted like snow on a spring day when she heard Anne's words to George Harville. It gave her the courage to take a fresh sheet of paper and pour out her feelings.

"I meant every word I wrote," Freddie told her as they admired a rack of old quilts. "You've never been supplanted. I've never loved anyone but you. I've never seen your equal. I meant to forget you, tried to forget you, maybe even deluded myself into thinking that I was over you. But when I thought I had achieved indifference, I was merely angry. When you told me you were worried about my career, I only blamed the influence of your family and friends, and denied the honesty and validity of your concerns."

"If we were found out, it would have been the end of your career,"

Anne said, her brow wrinkling with worry. "That's still true, isn't it?"

Freddie stopped to look down at her, and caressed her cheek with the back of her hand. "You never did pay a lot of attention to the news, did you? The death knell of Don't Ask, Don't Tell happened when the people elected Barack Obama last November. It's going to take some time, but he's working on it. The Joint Chiefs of Staff don't exactly do things with lightning speed, then it has to get approved by Congress. They don't move all that quickly, either. But give it a couple of years, and it'll be over, and I'll be able to serve openly as who I really am. I'll probably be able to claim you as my significant other, you'll even qualify for benefits."

"You're dreaming," Anne laughed at her. "That sounds too impossible to be true."

"We live in an impossible world," Freddie answered. "After all, everyone seemed to think that I was romantically interested in Louis, which seems crazy while you were in the same room."

"Well, even I was uncertain, and I know you pretty well," Anne reminded her.

"I was lonely, and being with the Musgrove boys put me close to you. I never meant for anyone to misconstrue my intentions," Freddie told her ruefully. "But during the accident, I realized everyone in the family, and the Harvilles, and the people at the hospital were treating me like a girlfriend. I was shocked, and so I beat a strategic retreat. My brother Edward had been complaining that he hadn't gotten to see me yet, so instead of seeing you one last time on Christmas Eve, I spent the holidays with him. Afterwards, I texted both boys to say that I was too busy at work, and I was sorry I didn't have any more free time to come to New York."

"How is Edward?" Anne asked. "He was nice. I remember when he came to see you at Cornell."

"He's wonderful, he loves living in Pittsburgh, and I can see why. If there was an Air Force base there, I would put in to get stationed there in a heartbeat," Freddie told her. "It's such a neat city. You'll have to go with me next time I visit him. He asked after you."

"He did?" Anne was surprised.

"You and I were pretty thick together when he visited. I hadn't told him about us then, but he suspected. And he wanted to know if I was still in touch with you, since of course it's been a lot of years since college. I told him I'd reconnected with you by chance, and you were every bit as smart and lovely as you were then."

Anne smiled, pleased by Freddie's bias. "Well, I don't know. I've seen college photos of myself, I looked awfully good back then."

Freddie paused as they were walking through an entire display case with nothing but antique Coca Cola paraphernalia. "I hope you don't mind my asking, but have you been losing weight since I first saw you again?"

Anne nodded. "A little over sixty pounds."

"Good for you! I know losing weight is hard," Freddie congratulated her.

"You made it easy. Louis told me you'd barely recognized me. I looked at myself in the mirror that night, and decided I didn't like what I saw. It was the first time I'd cared about my health or what I looked like since the day I broke up with you," Anne told her.

"You know I love you no matter how much weight you gain or lose," Freddie told her gently.

Anne touched her arm. "I know. You are much kinder than my family. And maybe that's why you made me care about myself, when all their nagging couldn't make me care."

"Do you think we'll be able to tell your family now? Or do we need to keep this a secret?" Freddie asked.

"I'm not 19 anymore," Anne told her stoutly. "They can't persuade me or bully me into thinking our love is wrong, like they did when I was young and more easily swayed by their opinions."

"It was hell, watching you sit at the restaurant before the George Carlin show, with all your family, all those people who don't like me, and who were clearly trying to set you up with William Elliot. Are you convinced they'd accept us now?" she reiterated her question tenderly.

"Well," Anne smiled mischievously, "not everyone wanted to set me up with William. My sister is convinced she wants him for herself. And having witnessed Penny Clay with William on the street in the Oregon District when both of them were supposed to have other plans, I can't help but wonder if there are two people under the same roof with me who are interested in keeping him for themselves. As for William, I would speculate he likes to be a 'player.' So my family is demonstrating all around poor character judgment. And you can lump Lanie Russell in with the rest of them as part of my family. She was as eager as the rest for me to start dating William."

"I think she had more influence on you than your father and sister. Is she still going to be convinced that what we have is sinning against God and nature, and insist that we split up?"

"Well, here's where I will be putting her love for me to the test. I gave you up because I trusted her, and I loved her for trying to fill in for my mother ever since she died. Leaving you practically destroyed me. I think she knows that. She's had to watch me all these years. If she loves me, she'll have to accept me for who I am, and you because you're the one I chose." Freddie put her arm around her, and squeezed, while she continued, "I know who I am now, and what I want. She tested my love for her, now it's my turn to test her love for me. I hope she passes it. I don't know what the outcome will be. But if she makes me choose between the two of you again,

I'm not making the same choices I did last time."

"That's my brave girl," Freddie said, and kissed her behind a giant cabinet of silver plates and candlesticks.

CHAPTER 28

Anne drove home in a cloudy haze of happiness. In one morning, her life, her entire universe, had changed. She walked through the door in a dream, talked with Mary, and Charles, and Henry, who all treated her as if she was the same person who had run out the door mere hours ago. The caterers treated her as if she was just another person they were working for. When her father and Elizabeth got home, they talked to her as if nothing was different.

When she went up to her room to change for the party, she grabbed a pillow off her bed, flopped into the big chair in her room in front of the window, hugged it to herself, and giggled. She finally allowed herself to smile, really smile, a full, face-splitting, soul-revealing, joyous smile.

Freddie loved her! She had always loved her. The whole time Anne was wondering in agony if Freddie was interested in pursuing something romantic with one of the Musgrove boys, Freddie was coming around just to be near her. She buried her face in the pillow, and screamed with joyous rapture.

By some miracle of circumstance, she had a new dress for the party. She usually wore the baggy sweater dresses and tunics with spandex leggings that every girl had in her closet. But this new sundress had a cute asymmetric neckline, with one shoulder left bare. It made her feel a little bit like the statue of a Greek goddess. The skirt was narrow, too, and the way the fabric was gathered in on one side was very flattering, and emphasized the fact that there was a lot less of her now than when she had first laid eyes on Freddie again.

When she came down to the party, which was spread out in the three-season porch and spilled out onto the patio by the pool, her father and Vic Dalrymple had already availed themselves of the little catering buffet. Miss Carteret and Elizabeth were taking their turn serving themselves, with the

Wallises immediately behind them awaiting their turn. Charles and Mary and Henry were beaming, which Anne took to mean that they had been introduced to one of the richest men in America. Vic paused as he was about to pass her. "Good evening, Anne. You are looking particularly fetching tonight. Is that a new shade of lipstick?"

"New dress," she told him, and the smile she gave him was a sincere one.

"Well, you look smashing in it," he told her approvingly.

Her father, trailing along in Vic's wake, had to stop and give her an appraising look. "You do look particularly well this evening, Anne. Whatever it is you're doing, you should keep it up. Are you using a new moisturizer or something?"

"No, father, just making a lot of use of our pool, and the country club membership."

"Well, your skin looks much improved, somehow. The benefits of exercise, right?" he left to follow Vic to a seat at the table, where the *Say Anything* game was placed tantalizingly in the middle.

When William Elliot arrived and gave her more of his elaborate and sexually-charged compliments, she could only pity him. "Really, William, can you manage to talk to a woman without getting crude?"

"Depends on what that woman is wearing, I think," he said, and grinned at her cleavage in what Anne imagined he thought was his most seductive manner.

It was a relief when the doorbell rang, and Anne admitted Captains Harville and Wentworth. "Am I glad to see the both of you," she sighed happily.

"Why, what's wrong?" Freddie asked casually, but her eyes looked concerned.

"I just like you two more than anyone else that's going to be at this little party tonight. And George, I think you're a better bartender than my father. I need a drink, if you're up to fixing something yummy?"

"With pleasure!" George limped forward with energy toward the bar, leaving Anne alone with Freddie for a delicious moment.

They kissed, and Freddie looked earnestly into her face. "Are you all right?"

Anne looked at Freddie with a face full of love. "Whenever you're with me, I'm more than all right."

As they walked in to join the party, she noticed Penny slipping out of the room, and William following soon behind her. "Go on and get a drink and some food," she told Freddie. "I'll be along in a minute."

Whatever imp of the perverse took hold of her, she was curious enough about William and Penny's behavior to investigate. While she had no interest in William, if he was playing around with both Elizabeth's and

Penny's affections at the same time while also hitting on her, she felt it was her duty as a sister to find out, and let Elizabeth know if her best friend was fooling around with the man she was interested in.

"Did you get me the names?" she heard William ask from the kitchen.

"Not yet," Penny answered.

"Why not?" she could hear the impatience in William's voice.

"If you think it's so easy spying on people, you do it yourself," Penny snapped at him.

"I'm paying you pretty darned well to get me that information," William snapped back. "The vain old asshole can't be that difficult to get a few names from."

"Like I said, if you think you can do it faster and better, do it yourself," Penny repeated. "It's not like I've been able to get his computer password yet. I keep trying, but he's not as dumb as he looks, you know. Not every guy passes over all his trade secrets the moment he starts having sex with a person."

Anne thought of sneaking back down the stairs, but the imp of the perverse still had firm control over her impulses. She loudly ascended the last two steps, and bustled into the room. "Oh, good, Penny, you're here. Don't we have a couple more ice buckets somewhere? Captain Harville says we should have more ice on hand by the bar."

Both of them jumped when she appeared, and stared at her guiltily. Penny stammered, "I thought they were all out there already."

"He probably didn't see them. But just in case, where do they usually live? You're the one who knows where everything is in this house," Anne laughed lightly.

Penny opened one of the cabinet doors, and to Anne's relief, there was an ice bucket on the shelf. "There we go. Captain Harville isn't completely unobservant." She grabbed the ice bucket, filled it from the dispenser on the front of the refrigerator, and scurried out of the room.

Corporate espionage, so that's the game, Anne thought to herself. Well, it was nice to know she was a decent judge of character, after all. She had to wonder how long Penny Clay and William Elliot had known each other. Which came first, Penny's friendship with Elizabeth and then William, or her relationship with William? Was she recruited after she had become a fixture in the household, or beforehand? It made sense out of William's motivations for repairing his relationship with her father. She had never really been able to believe it had been merely because he'd missed his old mentor.

George looked a little surprised when Anne handed him the ice bucket in exchange for the glass he handed her. "Just in case we need more ice," Anne volunteered.

"Well, then, you'd better make an announcement that the bar is open,"

George told her. "There is already a huge bucket of ice right here, people are going to need to do a lot more drinking."

The board game was much better than Anne would have anticipated. Instead of the usual sort of games that were a matter of competition, the cards were merely questions to encourage discussion on a large variety of topics. There were too many people for one game, so they were divided into multiple tables, with multiple games.

Anne and Freddie maneuvered to be at the same table together, playing *Say Anything*. Some of the questions were funny, like answering what would be most entertaining to see thrown off a tall building. Some were fairly thoughtful, like discussing the most important technology of the past century. The most profound for Anne was the question asking what one thing you would change about your own past. "My decisions," Anne had answered. "My pride, which kept me separated from the person I valued most," Freddie had written. When the judge showed everyone the different answers, they had locked eyes across the table. Each knew what the other had written, and a perfect understanding flowed between them.

CHAPTER 29

Who can be in doubt of what followed? What force in the universe is more powerful than two young people in love? Especially two people not so young that external forces could drive them apart through force or other persuasions.

The possible imprudence of their relationship, with regards to Freddie's career, was vastly reduced a little over a year after they took an apartment together. The year 2010 was filled with almost monthly news on the repeal of Don't Ask, Don't Tell, and by July of the following year, President Obama, the Secretary of Defense, and the Chairman of the Joint Chiefs of Staff sent certification to Congress, officially ending Don't Ask, Don't Tell on September 20th. Freddie was able to continue her service in the Air Force openly as a lesbian.

Anne's family greeted her renewal of her relationship with Freddie somewhat lukewarmly, but without the hostility of the past. Freddie's income as a test pilot was such that Walter could not object to the lifestyle Anne would be able to live, and Elizabeth was indifferent to any behavior of Anne's. Both of them felt an obligation to Anne for uncovering the espionage attempts of Penny and William, and yet instead of the incident drawing the family closer together, father and daughter seemed to blame Anne as the bearer of bad tidings and the agent responsible for separating them from their sycophants. As disingenuous as the admiration had been, they missed having two admirers to fawn over them, and it was Anne's fault that they were gone.

Anne didn't have too much trouble convincing them that she should move out, and removing her presence from the household may also have helped put Freddie in a favorable light with her parent and sibling. Freddie was the means by which her absence was achieved. Her father was even fairly generous financially, paying off her car loan when he got a work bonus, and sending erratic but ample checks to assist with household finances or those random emergencies which inevitably visit people in the course of a lifetime. While he had little affection for Anne, she was still his daughter, and he still needed to act like a parent from time to time.

Mary, by contrast, was vastly pleased by Anne's situation. She had always been a fan of the TV show Ellen, and if Ellen DeGeneres could be a lesbian, how cool was it that her own sister was, too? It seemed highly fashionable, and something she could brag about to customers when they came to pick up their dry cleaning. She credited herself with having brought about the reunion of the lovers, since Anne was staying with her when Anne and Freddie first set eyes on each other again.

Charles and the rest of the Musgroves were, predictably, supportive and welcoming. Anne was only family by marriage, but they liked her exceedingly well, and they had all liked Freddie a great deal, and were quite thrilled by the thought of a romance blossoming right under their noses. Mrs. Musgrove insisted upon making a fairly generous wedding present when Anne and Freddie decided to go to Massachusetts for the weekend and get married.

Telling her father and sister caused trepidation enough, but Anne was shaking inside when she told Lanie Russell. She thought about not telling her at all, but since the rest of the family knew, Lanie was sure to find out. Lanie was the one who had been so insistent when breaking them up before, spouting Bible quotes and lecturing on the sins of her choice. Anne was forced into presenting Lanie with the truth, and waiting to see how she responded. She would either have a change of heart, or Anne would have to lose the second woman who had been a mother to her. For all her brave words to Freddie, she was very much afraid of what Lanie was going to do.

When she sat down at her webcam on the computer, she specifically excluded Freddie from the call. If it didn't go well and Lanie said hurtful things again, she didn't want Freddie knowing about it. She also insisted on telling her over video instead of by phone call. This conversation was too important not to do face to face.

After some initial chit chat, Anne took a deep breath and blurted it out. "Lanie, I need to let you know, Freddie and I are going to Massachusetts next weekend and getting married."

Lanie's face froze for a moment. "You're really sure this is what you want? You know it's going to make for a life of hardship. Most people do not think same-sex marriage is acceptable."

Anne had played this conversation in her mind over and over beforehand, imagining all possible permutations, and practicing her answers in front of the mirror. "I love her. She makes me happy. I haven't been happy since I broke up with her, now I get a second chance. Most people don't get a second chance."

Lanie sighed. "I thought maybe it was William Elliot who was causing such a transformation in you. But your father told me you discovered him and Penny Clay spying on him. I can only be relieved that you weren't in love with him. Being married to an Air Force Captain who is allowed to admit she's in a relationship with you is better than being married to a jerk who was using the family for who knows what."

Anne nodded. "A lot of people seemed to think I was interested in William. It's been a relief to tell them about Freddie, which convinces them I really mean it when I say I wasn't interested, so I'm not broken hearted about him."

Lanie looked intently at her through the webcam. "Anne, I was wrong. Completely wrong. Even my new minister at church says that homosexuality is not a choice, it's how God made people like you. I can see how happy you are, and I'm happy for you. I love you, and I'm sure I will come to love Freddie as much as any other partner you might have brought home. If you want me at your wedding, I will be there."

Of course Freddie's family and friends were all thrilled for them. Both George Harville and Jamie Benwick insisted they had known for years what Freddie's preferences were. The Crofts, Freddie's parents, and brother Edward all insisted upon coming up for the wedding. Anne felt it keenly that while their wedding party was small, it was almost entirely made up of Freddie's friends and family. Her only contributions to the circle of well-wishers were Lanie and Mrs. Smith, whose health had taken enough of a turn for the better that she was able to go back to working. She insisted upon spending her first paycheck on a plane ticket to Boston.

When she mentioned it to Freddie, she had a way of putting things into perspective, as she always did. "Does it matter? We're married. They're not your friends and your family, and my friends, and my family. They're our friends, and our family. Isn't that what marriage is about? Combining forces, because we are stronger together than we are apart?" She kissed Anne's forehead fervently. "Don't forget, I'm an officer in the U.S. military. It can be frightening at times, and there may be times and places where I can't take you with me. If I have to be separated from you, I know you'll be taken care of. I need to know you're being taken care of. The people who witnessed our wedding are the people who will be there, for the both of us."

Anne happily wrapped her arms around her wife. "So you're telling me that in my own way, being married to an officer, I'm serving my country, too?"

Freddie laughed and kissed her, on the mouth this time. "Well, you are."

Finis

ABOUT THE AUTHOR

Jeanette Watts is a dancer, a seamstress, an avid traveler, and a writer. She was attending a lecture at a JASNA conference that was discussing the fan fiction inspired by *Pride and Prejudice*, and the point was brought up that *Persuasion* does not lend itself well to modern rewrites because the themes are more dated. "No they aren't," was her immediate thought. "You just have to get the stakes right."

This novel is her attempt to get it right.

Her previous novel, *Jane Austen Lied to Me*, is a humorous tribute to all of Jane's fans, and all of her completed works. Her first two novels, *Wealth and Privilege* and *Brains and Beauty*, are a Yankee girl's homage to Margaret Mitchell, whose *Gone With the Wind* captured her imagination in 7th grade, and never let go.

Made in the USA
Lexington, KY
03 November 2019